Peril on the Oregon Trail

Hannah Henford, travelling West from Ohio with her family aboard a steamer on the Missouri River, meets the reticent Andrew Callahan, a young man also following the trail towards Oregon. The boat docks and during the next part of the journey, the strong and broad-shouldered Andrew captures the heart of Hannah with his bravery, and the two become close.

Jeremiah Smith, a mysterious and adventurous mountain man, discovers Hannah alone and takes her deep into the open in search of wild turkeys. Hannah cannot help but be charmed by Jeremiah, but he may not be all that he seems.

In Arapaho territory, Andrew will be needed again: he will face peril in pursuit of Hannah; he will face Peril on the Oregon Trail.

Peril on the Oregon Trail

Billy Hall

A Black Horse Western
ROBERT HALE

ISBN 978-0-7198-1866-0

The Crowood Press
The Stable Block
Crowood Lane
Ramsbury
Marlborough
Wiltshire SN8 2HR

www.crowood.com

Robert Hale is an imprint
of The Crowood Press

Typeset by Catherine Williams, Knebworth

Printed and bound in Great Britain by
CPI Group (UK) Ltd, Croydon CR0 4YY

CHAPTER 1

Hannah swallowed so hard it hurt her throat. Words scrambled together in a hopeless tangle in her mind, refusing to straighten out enough to escape her mouth. It was just not possible! Her parents were actually, seriously talking of leaving? Just picking up and leaving everything she knew, everything they had worked for, everything her future held? It was unthinkable! Beyond unthinkable!

The Ohio farm was small, but fertile. Wilbur Henford, her father, had done well with it. The crops were adequate, if not bountiful. His barn and fences were always kept well mended. The neighbors were agreeable. They had the necessities of life. In fact, they were quite comfortable. Why even think of leaving here?

'Will's growing up,' her father explained, his voice carefully patient. 'He's going to be wanting to set out on his own in a few years. Most of the land around here is long since taken up. We don't have any part of the means to just out-and-out buy land to expand the farm.'

'It wouldn't have to be right next to ours.'

'That's another good point,' her father went on. 'What do you mean by "ours"?' You don't expect to sit home and be an old maid, helping with your parents' farm your whole life, do you?'

'At least I don't think that's what Ethan has in mind,' young Will interjected, his mischievous eyes twinkling.

Hannah flushed bright red. 'Will, keep your mouth shut. I'm not that serious about Ethan anyway.'

'Well, he's that serious about you.' Will grinned. 'He's plannin' on findin' a way to buy old man Higgins's place when he's too old to farm it, seein' as how they ain't got no kids. Bud Higgins ain't getting' no younger, so that ain't gonna be long.'

'But ... but ... but what will we do with this place?'

'Lewis Lowenthal has already offered to buy us out. For a pretty fair price, actually.'

'But Oregon seems so terribly far away,' Frances's voice was wistful.

'It's a far piece, to be sure, Fannie,' her husband agreed. 'Pertnear two thousand miles from here. But with a good start it's easily made in one summer. And there's land a-plenty there. Good land. Better'n what we got here, even. And it can be had for a song or for nothin' at all, now. We can snap up enough land to have all we'll want for as long as we want it.'

'But ... but there's our cows and the horses and the pigs,' Hannah objected.

'We'll take our livestock with us. They'll trail along just fine. Even pigs keep up with a wagon train just fine, they tell me. We'll just pull up stakes and move, lock, stock and barrel.'

'Even my chickens?' Frances demanded, seeming to think of them for the first time.

'Even your chickens,' her husband assured her.

'Especially your chickens, in fact. On the way, and after we get there, there'll be a premium on chickens and eggs both. You'll be able to do a lot better than pin money with them.'

The conversation quickly moved from 'whether' to 'when,' as if it had all been decided before Hannah was even consulted.

The next month was chaotic at best. Wilbur bartered for an excellent Conestoga wagon, with three extra wheels and one extra axle for both front and back. It was made by one of the best wagonwrights in the county. It was fitted with a false floor, beneath which they concealed the small trove of valuables that they prized. It was amazing how much furniture and boxed goods they could load into the conveyance, and still have room to sleep during bad weather. And the main body of the wagon was completely waterproof, so it would float when they forded rivers!

Wilbur also traded for four more head of oxen, larger than those they already owned, so he could spell the teams all the way westward. He had an extra box slung beneath the wagon for many bushels of oats to augment their feed when it became necessary. He had no intention of being among those who fell by the wayside for lack of foresight and good planning.

Close to the end of that month it seemed as if the family could talk of nothing else around the table. Suddenly unable to contain herself any longer, Hannah fled through the door. She ran all the way over the hill, across the small creek, and up the broad valley to the Landry farm. Ethan saw her coming and ran to meet her. They locked in a long embrace with her trembling in his arms.

'Feels like the time for you to leave is comin' up way too

fast,' he guessed.

'It seems like just yesterday when they first mentioned it. Now we're almost ready to leave!'

'They didn't give you much time to get used to the idea. I wondered when they'd finally get around to tellin' you,' Ethan commiserated as her trembling slowed.

'You knew before I did?'

'Yeah. I've knowed for a month or so longer 'n you have, I guess. They didn't want me sayin' nothin', though, till they was sure.'

'You knew, and you didn't say anything to me?'

'They asked me not to.'

'But you knew I'd want to know. I had a right to know. How could you do that?'

He looked at her, lost for an answer.

'How could you know something that important and not say a word?' she continued to demand. 'Do you think that's honest, to talk with me almost every day and just keep your mouth shut? Isn't that just the same as lying?'

'No, it ain't lyin' at all, if I don't say nothin'. Nobody tells everything they know.' He tried to wrap his arms around her again, but she twisted away from him.

'How could you do that?' she demanded again. 'If you truly loved me, you'd never keep something like that away from me.'

'But I do love you.'

'Well, I guess you're just going to have to get over it. We're leaving for Oregon in just over a week.'

'That don't mean it's over between us,' Ethan protested instantly. 'I've been thinking about this. There's wagon trains gettin' organized every year. I can find one that's just formin' up and get myself a spot in it, and I can come next year. We'll only be apart for a year, then we can start out together, out in Oregon. A brand new start, for a brand new couple, in a brand new land'

Hannah folded her arms across her chest. 'That sounds awfully cut and dried. Especially for two people that don't even have any kind of understanding between them.'

'But I thought we did … we do, I mean. I mean … I love you. You love me too, don't you?'

'Loving you and agreeing to be a couple, like we were engaged or something, are two different things, Ethan Landry.'

He stared at her, fumbling for words. 'But … but we could make it official. We can do that right now, Hannah. Hannah Henford, will you marry me?'

'Ethan, that's not fair. It's not a decent time or situation to even ask a question like that. Besides, when somebody asks me that, I want it to be romantic and deliberate, not just to win an argument standing out here beside … beside the corral, in a field of cow-pies, with a goat nuzzling me.'

Ethan swatted the goat, sending it on its way. Hannah was less than impressed.

'Oh, so that's all there is to it. Get rid of the goat and then it'll be all romantic! Well, you've got a lot to learn, Ethan, and I guess you're just going to have to learn it from someone besides me.'

She whirled and ran back toward her own house. Ethan called after her twice, but did not pursue her.

CHAPTER 2

A broad shoulder jostled her aside. There was no apology, no acknowledgement of any breach of etiquette. It was just a normal part of being on the overcrowded street of Independence, Missouri. It had been a long winter, with the congestion worsening daily as spring approached. She ignored it.

A crude hand took advantage of the closely packed throng to slide indecently along her left hip. She reacted with an instant elbow aimed at the offender. He merely chuckled as he faded away into the mass of hurrying bodies.

She uttered a sound as close to an expletive as she was likely to verbalize. Her father glanced aside at her.

'Problem?' he queried.

She shrugged. 'Just another indecent imbecile trying to cop a feel,' she groused.

Hannah, her younger brother and her father weaved their way through the crowds. Everybody seemed to be moving at a hectic pace, all heading in different directions, all intent on their own immediate goals. They ignored all else.

Independence was a prosperous young city in any season of the year. Now it was beyond any such mundane description. To say that it was crowded would be comically inadequate. Madhouse would have been far more apropos.

Even before the onset of winter hundreds of people, wagons and animals converged on the staging area for next spring's rush to head west on the Oregon Trail. The later in winter it drew, the greater the congestion. Available space quickly disappeared in town. Every week a new, wider circle of tents, crude huts, wagons and makeshift corrals seemed to emerge from the ground like a fungal growth surrounding the town. Independence was a dozen times its normal size.

Entrepreneurs, business people, crooks and drifters took advantage of the intense demand for goods of all kinds. Especially valuable were weapons, gunpowder and lead, grain, and staples that would keep through the winter and still be fresh in the spring.

Still a good month before the earliest and bravest of the wagon trains would form up and head west, the urgency to have all supplies laid by and preparations made was reaching fever pitch.

'I shouldn'ta let you come along,' Wilbur Henford groused. 'Earlier in the day it might not be so crowded. Things are already getting kinda rowdy.'

'I don't care, Father,' Hannah dismissed his concern. 'I'm so tired of being cooped up in that wagon or a tent all day I could scream.'

'There's a lotta really tough-lookin' characters, though,' young Will Henford fretted. 'Those guys look like they're about to get in a fight.'

One man hurrying to get somewhere jostled another too energetically, and was immediately shoved back in retaliation. Off balance, he whirled on the one who had pushed him, instantly sending a straight right fist to the man's jaw.

The other man reacted just as swiftly, sending a pair of blows of his own that sent his antagonist reeling. As that man caught his balance, he whipped a large knife from its sheath at his side. In the same motion he slashed out at the other man in a long sweeping arc.

As if he anticipated the action, the one being attacked

11

grabbed his attacker's arm, pulling him off balance, forcing the path of the knife to go wide. Even as he did he jerked his own Bowie knife from its sheath and buried it in his opponent's chest in one smooth action.

A look of shocked disbelief crossed the first man's face. He looked down at his chest, from which blood was pouring at a shocking rate. He looked back up into the face of the man who had bested him, as if trying to fathom how such a thing could happen. He sank to his knees, then fell forward onto his face in the deeply churned mud of the street.

Instantly two other men moved menacingly toward the man who had dispatched their companion. Just as quickly another man stepped up beside the one now being threatened. Every man held an 'Arkansas toothpick' low down and ready. Then a third man with a pistol at his hip stepped into the stand-off.

Wilbur and his two children were caught in the middle of the crush of people. They were much too close to what was apparently about to be a knife fight or gunfight between several parties, with no way to extricate themselves from harm's way.

Abruptly a large young man grabbed the three of them in an open-armed grip, as if trying to hug all three. He pushed them backward.

'Back up!' he commanded, his voice low but intense. 'Just keep backin' up. There's a gunsmith's shop right behind you. Keep backin' till we're inside. There's a sidewalk. Don't trip on it.'

Pushed along, almost falling, fighting to keep their balance, they were conveyed backward, away from the already growing fight in the street. The five participants were already surrounded by a crowd of people, shouting, jeering, urging them on, acting as if they had suddenly found themselves spectators at the center ring of a three-ring circus. So far the one armed with a pistol had not intervened.

Young Will tripped on the sidewalk as he backed into it, in spite of the warning. As he started to tumble backward a strong hand grabbed the front of his shirt and kept him upright. One breathless moment later they were through the door into the gunsmith's shop. Wilbur surveyed his children anxiously.

'Are you both all right?'

'I'm fine.'

'Yes, Father. What in the world are they fighting about?'

The young man who had hustled them away from the fray explained.

'They're from two different wagon trains that are both determined to be the first ones across the river when the ice is gone. They're just lookin' for an excuse to have a go at one another.'

'We owe you a very large debt of gratitude, young man,' Wilbur said. 'I think I should know you.'

'We met, but just barely,' the younger man acknowledged. 'I'm Andrew Stevenson. My family's in the same wagon train that you're makin' up with.'

'Ah, yes. Now I remember. Well, thank you. I wasn't at all sure how to get out of the middle of that situation.'

'Real quick, is the best way.' Andrew grinned.

'Can I help you folks?' the gunsmith asked.

Wilbur nodded. 'Yes, as a matter of fact. We were heading to your establishment when we got caught up in a rather violent dispute. Do you have any of the new self-contained cartridge firearms that Colt has issued?'

'Ah, yes, in fact I do. Are you interested in revolvers or rifles?'

'Well, both, actually. We're preparing to head to Oregon when our wagon train is ready, and it seems prudent to be well armed and well supplied with ammunition.'

'A wise attitude. Let me show you what I would recommend.'

As he began his sales pitch, Hannah looked around for their rescuer. He was gone. She felt a sudden and inexplicable sense of loss.

CHAPTER 3

April was such a … delicious month. That's just the right word, Hannah Henford decided. Delicious. She leaned over the rail of the ferry and watched the rushing brown water of the Missouri River push against the side of the craft.

There was nothing delicious about the river, she corrected herself. Spring run-off swelled it to more than a mile wide. Filled with trees, brush and debris, its water was rich brown with mud. It was no wonder it was called 'Big Muddy'.

She looked back at the receding shoreline with a heavy sigh. Until they actually started crossing the river she had held out hopes of her parents changing their minds. It was too late now.

When they left Ohio, Ethan had promised to wait for her, to come west to Oregon at his first opportunity, to love her for the rest of his life, but deep down she knew better. Absence may make the heart grow fonder, but it usually grows fonder of somebody closer. Oregon sounded nice, but it was such a terribly long way away.

They had wintered at Independence, Missouri, awaiting spring before starting west. Then three families of their group had become ill. They had only had twelve families in their group to start with. The wagon master, Frank Cross, had insisted their whole group was the bare minimum for safety. They had no choice but to wait until everyone was healthy.

So they watched while other wagon trains formed up and headed out. The earliest ones would use up the best of the grazing close to the trail for their livestock. Of course they would travel in the wetter weather of spring, making deep ruts in the trail itself. That would not only slow them down, it would leave behind a trail of ruts, not to mention a lot of trash and debris that those who followed would have to deal with.

Even so, April was so beautiful. As they disembarked on the western bank of the river she looked around. A profusion of wild flowers adorned the rolling hills. Even trampled and abused by prior groups, the grass valiantly reached upward, casting a magical green carpet over the countryside.

She looked back at the ferry, just disgorging its next load of those who would be her traveling companions for the trip to come. Her breath caught. Her eyes, by chance, met the bluest pair of eyes she had ever seen. They belonged to the very man who had shuttled them to the safety of the gunsmith's shop some weeks earlier. Now they were focused directly on her.

Emboldened by the distance between them, she quickly

appraised the owner of those bright orbs so impossible to ignore. It was much easier to do so here than it had been in that previous, desperate situation. They belonged to a tow-headed young man, very close to her own age, or maybe just a bit older. His shoulders were broad and thick. His nose had a slight hump in the center, just enough to give him an almost noble appearance. His mouth was generous and lips full. He had a slight smile on his face.

To her disappointment, his eyes did not remain in contact with hers. He seemed more intent on gauging the terrain. At his side an older version of himself had to be his father. The two were obviously talking quietly, but she could hear nothing of their conversation.

She sighed and went back to the task of getting a bucket of water from the river. She dipped it from a quieter little backwater along the bank. Her mother would insist on letting it settle for at least two hours, then pouring the clearer water slowly into another container, careful to not disturb the sediment in the bottom of the bucket. Then she would boil all the strained water before she would allow any of her family to drink it, or use any of it in her cooking. What they needed for washing and such things wouldn't get boiled. At least they had the barrels of water carefully filled from the wells in Independence, now lashed to the sides of their wagon. It would be used sparingly for the whole trip.

A sudden burst of loud voices snatched her attention. Two young men were engaged in a vehement argument of some kind. Neither could have been much more than sixteen or so, but they were full grown. Abruptly one of them slammed a fist into the other's chin, sending him sprawling.

The assaulted youth leaped to his feet and attacked his

adversary. They grappled together, each trying to get in a blow the other wouldn't manage to block. The man she had been watching strode swiftly to the pair. He grabbed each of them by a shoulder and forced them apart by pure force of brute strength. They both resisted momentarily, then settled in to glare at each other, still straining against his iron grip.

Once more she couldn't hear what was said. By the time the wagon master arrived to mediate the dispute, the young man appeared to have it at least temporarily resolved.

Who did he say he is? Hannah asked herself. *Andrew. That's it. Andrew something.* She would make it a point of finding out more about him.

CHAPTER 4

The first day on the trail covered less than half a dozen miles of the more than 1,900 that lay before them. Most of the day was spent in getting everyone organized, getting the unharnessed animals accustomed to moving along together, and each driver adjusting his or her speed to the wagon immediately in front.

At this stage of the trip they really didn't need scouts, but their wagon master insisted on them anyway, establishing the routines that would be life-and-death matters later on.

Life and death became realities much more swiftly than anyone had imagined. Early in the afternoon a red-headed driver of one wagon bailed off the driver's seat and ran forward, swiftly catching up with the wagon in front of him.

Without a word he leaped up and grabbed that driver, whipping him off the driver's seat with amazing strength.

The man was caught completely by surprise. He landed flat on his back, but leaped to his feet, face livid. He towered over the redhead, but his size failed to intimidate the shorter man in any way.

'What do you think you're doing?' he demanded. 'Who are you?'

The man accosting him thrust his chin forward. In spite of his short stature he was broad-shouldered and as Irish as a leprechaun. With an Irish temper on him too, it would seem.

'Sure an' you'll be findin' out who I am if you come that close to runnin' over me girl again!'

'What are you talking about?'

'My Mary was almost for bein' run over by the hind wheel o' your wagon back there,' the other yelled. 'Sure an' you better be for learnin' to drive that thing or I'll be teachin' you.'

'I can't see what's happening behind my wagon!' the object of his wrath protested. 'Maybe you'd best be teaching your girl to watch out for the wagons.'

The wagons behind them were forced to stop as the two argued. Heads poked out to the side, trying to see what was going on. Even people from those wagons immediately in front of the two started walking back to find out what was going on.

'Don't you be tellin' me how to raise my young 'uns, or I'll be teachin' you a thing or two.'

'So teach me, you sawed-off big-mouth!' Enos Smeltzer, the larger man, challenged.

The words were no sooner out of his mouth than Pat

Callahan's fist drove into his nose, sending a spray of blood splaying outward.

Barely fazed by the blow, Enos scored every bit as quickly with a right of his own that lifted the Irishman from his feet and sent him sprawling.

Pat sprang up from the ground as if he had landed on springs, plunging forward toward the other man. A strong pair of hands grabbed him by the shoulders, impeding his effort to attack his opponent.

At the same time another man stepped in front of Enos, holding up his hands. Watching Pat warily, Enos paused. The pounding hoofs of a running horse announced the approach of Frank Cross, the wagon master. As his horse slid to a halt the big, rangy wagon boss leaped to the ground.

'Here! Here! What's goin' on here?'

Pat glanced at the wagon master, then returned his glare to Enos. He pointed a finger at his opponent, his anger making the finger quiver and shake.

'Sure an' 'tis this big reckless German that's nearly killin' me girl,' he sputtered. 'That's what's for goin' on.'

Frank faced Enos. 'Enos,' he demanded, 'what happened?'

'I ain't got no idea, Frank,' Enos protested. 'First thing I knew this wild Irishman jumped up and jerked me off the driver's seat and flung me on the ground without sayin' a word. Then he accused me of almost running over his girl with the hind wheel of my wagon. I can't even see the back wheels when I'm in the driver's seat.'

Frank turned back to Pat. 'How did it happen, Pat?'

'Sure an' me girl was runnin' to catch up to her sister an' she tripped an' fell. The wagon wheel didn't miss 'er more'n a whisker. If she'da fell to the side just a hair more, she'd be for bein' carried away by the banshees right now, she would.'

With a voice straining to be slow and calm, Frank said, 'Well, Pat, if you were in the driver's seat of Enos's wagon, would you have been able to see her?'

Pat's eyes leaped back and forth between Enos and Frank. He cleared his throat, but said nothing.

Frank continued, 'When you ran up to Enos's wagon, did he see you coming?'

'O' course not,' Pat snorted. 'He didn't know I was this side o' Independence till I up an jerked 'im off that seat.'

In that same calm voice Frank demanded, 'If he couldn't see you coming, why should he have been able to see your girl?'

Pat opened his mouth several times, and closed it each time. Finally he said,

'Sure an' I thought me girl was dead when I saw 'er fallin',' he said. He appeared suddenly close to tears.

'I'm sure you did,' Frank agreed. 'And I'm sure it scared the liver out of you.' His voice rose in volume and took on a tone of authority. 'But I can't have people in this train climbin' one another's frame over something that isn't their fault. You hear me?'

Pat looked back and forth between the two men another time or two. He swiped the back of his hand across his nose, leaving a bloody streak across his face. Silence hung heavily as nearly two dozen people, who had gathered around in a circle, stared.

Frank did nothing to ease Pat's discomfiture, or to break the deafening silence.

At last Pat spoke. 'Could be I was bein' a mite hasty at that,' he conceded in reluctant tones.

'Could be you owe Enos an apology.' Frank's tone made it clear it was not a question.

Pat swiped a hand on his pants leg. He looked around, then looked back at Enos. He stepped forward and abruptly thrust out his hand.

''Tis sorry I'm bein', Enos. 'Tis me temper gets me in trouble at times.'

After a moment's hesitation Enos accepted the extended hand.

'Well the next time you get mad at me,' he said, 'at least yell before you go jerkin' me off the seat o' my wagon, would you?'

Not wanting either man to say enough to reignite their tempers, Frank raised his voice so as to be clearly heard by everyone.

'All right! Everybody back to your own wagons. We're already makin' precious little progress today. If we get slowed up any more I'll make you pitch camp in the dark.'

As he swung back on his horse everyone hurried back to their own wagon. In minutes the procession was once again inching its snail's pace westward.

CHAPTER 5

'Could you use some help?'

Andrew turned to see Hannah Henford walking toward him.

'You bet,' he responded. His joyous surprise momentarily

overcame his normal reticence.

She came up beside him, swinging her whole body back and forth as she walked in an overt attempt to appear casual.

'Your turn to keep track of everybody's livestock, huh?'

He nodded. 'Yeah. Actually, it's my favorite duty, so far.'

'I bet it wasn't as much fun last week.'

He grinned. 'I only had one day of it while it was raining. And I had my slicker.'

'What's a slicker?'

In his wisest, most mature voice he replied, 'It's just a raincoat, made for wearing on horseback.'

'Really?'

'Yeah. It's got a wide yoke on the shoulders, and it's split up part way, so when I'm on my horse it keeps both legs covered.'

'Oh, how wonderful!' she enthused. 'So you can be out in the rain all day and not get wet.'

'Well, not as wet as I would without it, that's for sure.'

'The rest are getting quite a ways ahead,' she noted.

The last wagon of the train was just passing, nearly a quarter-mile to their left.

'Yeah. I need to get 'em moving and catch up. I just wanted to let 'em eat as long as I could. There's a really good patch of grass here. The wagons that got an earlier start really have grazed off the good grass close to the trail.'

'Can I help you?'

'Sure. I'll start 'em moving, and you can watch along this side and keep any of 'em from tryin' to turn back. I'll do the same around on the other side.'

'I can do that. I almost always went out and drove the milk cows in at home.'

Without further discussion, Andrew stuck a foot in the stirrup and stepped up onto his horse. He approached the forty-odd head of cattle and horses. Swinging a length of his lariat in a big circle he let out a shrill whistle.

'Heyah!' he yelled. 'Heyup, there. Get movin'. Heyup, heyup!'

At first the busily eating animals just looked up at him, then they resumed their eating. As he drew closer some of them turned and began to trot away from him. He aimed the whirling rope so it caught the ears of a cow that had refused to move. She whirled and lunged away, slowing to a walk after half a dozen lengths.

That seemed to be the signal to the others that they were going to have to obey. In a group they began to move away from the plentiful meal.

One brindle cow turned aside, abruptly deciding to circle around and return to the green grass. Hannah yelled at her, flapping her arms up and down, running to intercept her. The cow acted as if she intended to defy this new person's authority, then turned and lumbered back into the moving herd.

A dun horse decided it was the perfect opportunity. He turned away from Hannah and began to run on a course intended to outflank Andrew. Instantly Andrew stood up in his stirrups, leaned forward and yelled at his horse. His mount had already spotted the errant equine. He leaped forward, breaking into a full run almost instantly. It was no contest. Andrew's horse swiftly cut off the dun mare's intended path and turned her back into the herd as well.

Hannah stood watching, entranced by the scene. Andrew seemed to be at one with the animal he rode. His rope never stopped whirling. When his horse ran really fast his hat brim blew up in front, flat against the crown. He leaned forward, looking to her like a picture of a wild cowboy she had seen on the cover of a dime novel. Her parents would have been scandalized to know she had ever read such a thing.

Andrew veered his horse away from the herd and raced in a wide circle back around and over to where Hannah stood, full of admiration.

He didn't need to run. There just wasn't any way he was going to miss the chance to show off a little to a beautiful young woman. He brought the beast to a stop close beside her. He jumped down.

'There's always at least one that's just gotta see if he can get away without mindin',' he observed.

'Will they keep moving now?'

He nodded. 'Usually they do. The first couple days out they were kinda hard to keep together. They've pretty well got it figured out now, though.'

'Once they all learn, it'll be a lot easier.'

'Yeah. Some of 'em are always a lot harder to control than others.'

They walked together, comparing notes on some of the families in the group. They had to walk fast to keep up with the livestock, so they didn't talk nearly as much as either wanted. Andrew suddenly felt as if he were being rude.

'Do you wanta ride a ways?' he asked. 'You gettin' tired?'

'No. I'm fine.'

'You do know how to ride, don't you?'

'Sure.'

'Well, go ahead an' ride awhile. I don't mind walking.'

'Andrew! I'm wearing a dress. '

He frowned. 'You can't ride in a dress? Buster's gentle. Your dress won't spook 'im.'

She knew her cheeks were crimson, but she couldn't help it. She countered by giving her voice a scolding tone.

'I'm not going to climb on a horse in a dress and show my legs, for Pete's sake,' she said. He pondered the idea for a moment.

'OK. Tell you what. I'll hold Buster's bridle an' look straight ahead while you get on. Then you can get your dress pulled down afore I look around.'

She hated blushing like she knew she was.

'Promise you won't look?'

'Promise,' he said. He took his place at his horse's head, holding the side of the bridle, looking steadfastly away.

She pulled her dress up enough to allow her foot to reach the stirrup. She swung easily into the saddle. Quickly she pulled the dress down on both sides, making sure her legs were well covered. The tops of her high, laced boots were clearly visible, but she was properly and modestly covered.

'OK. You can look now.'

'Uh-oh,' Andrew said, pointing.

Following his point, she saw a big dappled steer turn back from the rest of the herd.

'I'll get him' she volunteered.

She lifted the reins and kicked the horse's sides. The horse knew his job well. He had already spotted the wayward animal. He leaped forward, racing to turn him back.

Hannah desperately grabbed for the saddle horn, surprised at the speed with which Buster accelerated. All she could think of for a moment was how mortified she would be if she fell off Andrew's horse when he had just talked her into riding him.

By the time she regained both her balance and her aplomb the horse had already accomplished what she had intended to do. The steer was persuaded of the error of his ways and rejoined his companions. She trotted back to where Andrew watched, a wide grin on his face.

'Hey, you did that like you knew what you were doing,' he complimented. 'Not bad for a girl.'

She wasn't sure whether he were serious or kidding. She glared appropriately for either case, and held her peace. *What do you mean, 'for a girl'? Besides, why do I suddenly care so much what he thinks?* she asked herself.

She watched him sidelong, trying to keep him from noticing. He walked with such a strong stride. His shoulders were so broad. For just a moment she felt as if she were being unfaithful to the memory of Ethan, the young man in Ohio. She shook her head impatiently. He was just part of the world she had left behind. Now everything was new and ... and ... well, adventurous. Yes. That was the word. Adventurous. *I wonder if Andrew feels at all attracted to me, or is he just being polite?* she pondered.

CHAPTER 6

A child's scream never bodes well.

Five children played boisterously together. They ran through the wild flowers. They chased an occasional butterfly. They made up games of tag or whatever else exuberant young minds might invent. Their squeals and peals of laughter lent an almost festive air to the sunny day.

Mothers kept a watchful eye. They were often able to see only the top halves of their children in the tall grass, but they were close. They hadn't considered danger that might be lurking out of sight, next to the ground.

Mary Callahan was six. She was fast on her feet.

'Sure an' she runs like a deer, the girl does,' her father often fondly noted. In fact, she easily outran even the children three and four years older than herself. Dress billowing behind her, red hair streaming in the wind, she exuded health and zest for life.

She looked back over her shoulder to see how close her pursuer was. She stepped on something. It moved beneath her foot. Instantly pain shot through her toe. She screamed. She whirled and kicked. A rattlesnake disengaged from her foot and landed in the grass. It slithered away and was immediately lost from sight.

'What happened?' an older boy shouted.

'It bitted me! It bitted me!' Mary screamed, continually kicking the offending foot as if to kick the pain away.

'What bit you?'

'A snake. It bitted me. Owie! Owie! It hurts!'

Though scarcely three years older than she, the boy scooped her up in his arms and ran toward the wagons, yelling at the top of his voice,

'Mrs Callahan! Mrs Callahan! Mary done got bit by a snake.'

By the time the lad reached the trail the wagons had all been jerked to a halt. Pat and Lydia Callahan both leaped from the seat of their wagon.

'Sit down, baby,' Pat ordered the girl.

Tears streaming down across the freckles that bridged her nose, Mary kept saying between sobs,

'It hurts, Daddy. It hurts. Make it stop hurting.'

Pat ripped the child's shoe and long stocking off. Twin fang punctures were clearly visible on her big toe.

Until the child screamed, a sense of security and well-being had settled over the entire wagon train. Everything had gone exceedingly well, with only one incident since they had ferried across the river and begun their long trek.

Andrew had hurried ahead of his family's wagon, fishing for an excuse he could use when he caught up to the Henfords' wagon. He hoped Hannah would be riding in front, or maybe driving the team, so he could talk with her without admitting he just wanted an excuse to see her. He had only had a couple chances to do so since they left Independence. He really wanted to get to know her better. Obviously she felt the same, or she wouldn't have sought him out when he was herding the livestock.

Luck was with him. Frances, Hannah's mother, was driving, and Hannah was sitting beside her. Hannah smiled broadly as Andrew came into view beside them.

'Oh, hi, Andrew,' she called out to him. 'Are you lost?'

'Yeah' he replied, grinning. 'Would you take me by the hand and lead me back to my wagon?'

'No!' she said, in pretended exasperation. Her eyes belied the tone of her voice completely. 'If you can't find your own way back you're just out of luck.'

Just then the ruckus erupted from near the Callahan's wagon. Instinctively Andrew whirled and ran toward it. He didn't even notice Hannah jump down from her own wagon and follow him. People were quickly gathering around.

'Sure an' we been knowin' about the rattlesnakes,' Pat lamented loudly. 'I thought they was farther west. We'd not a-been lettin' 'er run an' play in the grass if we'd been knowin'. O Lord o' heaven, Lord o' heaven, what're we gonna do? I thought they was all farther west.'

A man called loudly, 'Anyone know what to do for snakebite?'

'Frank'd know,' another replied, mindful of the wagon master's knowledge and experience, 'but he's off up ahead with the scouts.'

'I've heard what to do,' another offered. 'Never seen it done.'

'Sure an' what is it?' Pat pleaded. 'We gotta be knowin' an' quick.'

'I've heard you gotta cut it, where it's bit. Then you gotta suck the poison out.'

'Suck it out? With what?'

'Well, with your mouth, I guess.'

'But won't that poison you just as much?'

'I don't know. I guess you spit it out.'

'Sure an' it'll be for bleedin' if you cut it.'

'That's part o' what it's supposed to do. Then you suck the blood an' poison out together.'

'What if you're not for gettin' it all spit out?'

'I dunno. That's just what I heard somebody say.'

Andrew stepped forward, pulling a knife from its sheath at his belt. He looked at Pat and Lydia Callahan.

'You want me to try it?' he asked.

The couple looked at each other, then back at their sobbing daughter. She was twisting and writhing in her father's grip, obviously in great pain.

'Sure an' give 'er a try,' Pat said. 'We gotta try somethin'.'

Andrew dropped to his knees. Holding the child's foot in his hand he sliced the toe just above the marks of the fang. In his excitement he cut deeper than he intended. It began to bleed freely. He dropped his knife, leaned forward, and stuck her toe in his mouth. He sucked as hard as he could, feeling the warm rush of blood into his mouth. Along with it a sharp bitterness assailed his tongue. He turned his head and spewed the mouthful out on the ground. At the edges a greenish-gray substance streaked the bright-red fluid.

He plunged the toe back into his mouth and repeated the process. Then he did it again. Then again. Half a dozen times he repeated it.

He rocked back on his heels gasping for breath. The oldest member of the wagon train stepped forward. He spat a brown streak of tobacco juice on the ground.

'I heard tell chewin' tobaccy helps too.'

'Chewing tobacco?' Lydia demanded.

The oldster nodded. 'Works like a poultice, I've heard. Ain't never had occasion to try it on snakebite, but it works on wounds, some. It couldn't hurt.'

Once again Pat and Lydia looked at each other. Seeing the unspoken concurrence in each other's eyes, they both nodded.

'Sure an' it couldn't be hurtin' the child,' Pat consented.

Instantly the old-timer reached a finger into his mouth. From between his cheek and his permanently brown teeth he extracted a large wad of well-chewed tobacco. He handed it to Andrew as though he were, somehow, in charge.

Why do I have to be the one to do this? Andrew thought.

Stifling his revulsion, he grabbed the wet, sticky brown wad. He stuck it on Mary's toe, wrapping it around the digit. The flow of blood had already stopped.

'I need something to wrap around it, to keep it there,' he said.

Lydia ran to their wagon and came back almost at once with a handkerchief. Andrew wrapped it around the toe and tied it in a knot.

The clatter of running hoofs turned everybody's attention to the trail. Frank Cross and one of the outriders hauled their horses to a stop in a cloud of dust. Frank leaped from the saddle.

'Who got snakebit?' he demanded.

Pat pointed at his daughter. 'Sure, 'twas me little one, Frank. An' not a one of us knowin' what to do, even.'

'Real odd to run onto rattlers this far east,' Frank said, 'or I'd have talked about it. Best thing to do is bleed it. Suck the poison out if you can. Then put a poultice on it. Chewin' tobaccy is about the best. That or fresh cow manure.'

'Sure an' that's what the lad here already done,' Pat replied.

Frank's eyes jerked to Andrew. 'You cut it and sucked the poison out?'

'Yessir.'

'You put a poultice on it?'

'Yessir. I put a cud of tobacco on it.'

'Where's a lad like you get chewin' tobacco?' the group's leader demanded.

Andrew waved a hand toward the old-timer. 'It was Mr Anderson's. He said to use it.'

'Did you bleed it good?'

'Yessir. I think so.'

'How many mouthfuls o' blood?'

'Uh … I … I'm not sure. Five or six.'

Frank nodded. 'That should be enough, if you were quick enough. Seconds count with snakebite.'

He turned back to the frantic family. He brushed a hand across the girl's head.

'It's gonna hurt. Her leg's gonna swell up bad. Ain't nothin' else we can do, though.'

'Will … will she be all right?' Lydia asked hesittantly. Frank glanced quickly at the girl, then back at her parents.

'Yeah. Yeah. Sure she will. She'll be fine.'

Pat's eyes flashed fire briefly. 'Don't you be lyin' to me girl, Frank. Tell it to us straight.'

Frank took a deep breath, trying not to focus on the child's pleading eyes.

'I can't tell you that. Sometimes folks get by with just a real sore hand or leg or somethin' for a while, and it heals up and goes away and they're fine. Sometimes folks lose the arm or the leg. Sometimes gangrene sets in. Sometimes they … they just don't make it. I wish I could give you more encouragement. There's just no way to know.'

Pat and Lydia moved closer together, hovering over their child, whom Pat now held in his arms.

'Keep her warm and pray a lot,' Frank said. 'If you happen to have it, a couple or three tablespoons of brandy will help the pain and let her sleep.' He shifted his attention to the circle of frightened and concerned faces around him.

'After this, if you let the kids go off playin' like that, make sure they got a dog or two with 'em. Any good dog'll either kill a snake or raise a ruckus enough to keep the kids away from it.'

He mounted his horse and rode away. Only the hunch of his shoulders betrayed the burden that bore down on him. *I shoulda warned 'em earlier,* he scolded himself.

The Callahans carried Mary to their wagon and made her as comfortable as possible. Andrew carefully cleaned the blade of his knife and slid it back into its sheath. As he walked past the Callahan's wagon, he heard Lydia praying aloud.

He jumped as a hand was laid on his arm. He jerked his head around. Hannah stood beside him, the fingers of her hand resting tentatively on his arm.

'Oh, Andrew, that was the finest, bravest thing I have ever seen anybody do in my life. If Mary lives she will owe her life to you.'

Andrew struggled for words, feeling himself flush scarlet.

'I ... I just didn't know what else to do,' he said. 'I had to do somethin'.'

'Do you feel all right?' Hannah asked. 'It won't make you sick, will it?'

At the time, Andrew hadn't allowed himself to worry about that. He was making up for it now. He shrugged his shoulders, making the best show of manly courage he could manage.

'Just have to wait an' see,' he said. Abruptly the fear in his eyes was replaced by a spark of a different nature.

'Maybe you'd oughta stay real close to me, though, just in case.'

Hannah giggled. She gave him a playful shove. She turned and began to walk quickly to catch up to her family's wagon. As his own wagon caught up to him, Andrew realized his mind was filled more with Hannah's face than Mary's.

CHAPTER 7

'Is her leg any better?'

Hannah took a deep breath. 'I think so. She's not as sick as she was. She's eating the soup her mother makes for her. Her leg is still three times the size it should be, and all purple. It doesn't really look as bad as it did a couple days ago, though.'

Relief was evident in Andrew's voice. 'It's not gettin' any worse, anyway, huh?'

'No. It's some better.'

By the following Sunday Mary was markedly better. Frank insisted that the train should find a good campsite on Saturdays, as they did not move on Sundays. He insisted that both men and animals needed a day of rest. They'd get to Oregon quicker if they 'paid heed to what the good Lord taught us.'

Accordingly, Sunday was something of a holiday. The early part of the day was devoted to checking wagons, harnesses, yokes, guns, and everything else upon which their lives depended. Necessary repairs were made. Later on, wheels would probably need to be replaced occasionally. Frank had insisted that every wagon must have at least one spare front wheel and one spare hind wheel. Most had more than one spare.

Instead of each family fixing their own meals on Sundays, they had a common meal, late in the day. While the meal was cooking Lars Gullickson would bring out his squeeze box and Pat would get out his fiddle, and they would have a church service of sorts. It began with the singing of hymns.

Then Frank or somebody he selected would stand and read a segment of scripture. In the same manner someone was selected to offer thanks for the food and petitions for their safety. By the time these observances had run their course the food was usually ready. They would eat their fill and some extra.

The Pilgrims would have been scandalized, however, at the wagon train's customary course from that point on. The musicians picked up their instruments again. The music selection would drift into songs that weren't religious in nature. The longer it continued, the livelier the music became. By the time Pat whipped out 'Turkey in the Straw' folks were dancing to the music. It was a wonderful break from the monotony and constant vigilance of the trail.

As the singing started that Sunday Mary Callahan was lifted down from their wagon. Moving slowly and limping heavily, she none the less walked from the wagon to where everyone was gathered. As soon as someone spotted her a shout went up. People started clapping their hands. Men whooped. Women cried. Mary was pale, thin and drawn, but she was alive and on two feet.

'She looks like death warmed over, sittin' on a tombstone, with both feet a-danglin' in the grave,' Ole Anderson muttered softly to Hildegard as he laid his squeeze-box aside. 'Hilda' as everyone knew his wife, elbowed him sharply in the ribs.

'That's not funny, Ole,' she scolded in a harsh whisper.

'It was my tobaccy what kept 'er alive,' he asserted.

'Well, maybe it's been worth me putting up with it all these years, then,' she responded.

'It's what keeps me alive too,' Ole opined.

'Am I supposed to be thankful about that?'

'Ya better be. You don't know where I hid our money.'

'Is that what you think? Well, don't be surprised when you go lookin' for it, and find out it isn't where you hid it.'

Suddenly oblivious to everything else around them, he whirled to his wife. He forgot to keep his voice down so that only his wife could hear.

'Did you find that money?'

'Keep your voice down. Folks are looking.'

He leaned over close. His whisper could only be called a quieter shout.

'Did you?'

She straightened her dress over her legs, which were extended on the ground. She shrugged.

'What do you think?'

Wilbur Henford leaned over and whispered in his wife's ear.

'Wanta make a bet on whether it's right where he put it, and she's just waitin' till he goes runnin' to check, so she'll know where it is?'

Frances – whom everyone knew as Fannie – tried to stifle her giggle.

'I think she just wants to torment him. There are only so many places you could hide it in a wagon.'

'Unless he had a false bottom built into it, like we did. Then he'd have to empty the wagon clear out to get at it.'

She giggled again. 'Do you think we just might all notice if he did that?'

'That means Ole's gotta go clear to Oregon afore he knows whether Hilda's got their money.'

Fannie actually snorted in her effort to keep from

laughing. 'Oh, poor Ole!'

'Serves the old tightwad right.'

It was Fannie's turn to place a jab of a well-practiced elbow in her husband's ribs. 'Will! It's Sunday. Be nice.'

'Yes, dear. But tomorrow it'll serve the old tightwad right.'

Fortunately, their conversation and those of most of the other families close to the Andersons were drowned out by all the celebration of Mary's appearance. She stayed with the group for nearly an hour before she was obviously exhausted. Her father picked her up and carried her back to the wagon. The fact that she was going to recover without losing her leg lent a festive mood to the rest of the day.

As Pat returned he stopped in front of Andrew. The young man and Hannah had managed to sit beside each other in a way that appeared that each was sitting with their own family. It was the third Sunday in a row on which they had done so. Each week they sat a little closer to each other and a little further from their families. Everybody appeared not to notice. Pat addressed Andrew.

'Young man, I'm for just wantin' to thank you one more time. Sure an' 'twas your quick actin' that saved that wee girl o' mine. The banshees woulda come for her as sure as anythin' had you not. I'll be forever grateful to ye.'

Clearly embarrassed, Andrew mumbled, 'It was somebody else who told me what to do. I didn't know.'

'It was my tobaccy, I'm tellin' ya,' Ole insisted.

Several people laughed. Pat turned to Ole, ''Tis only fair, then, when I have the chance to be payin' ye back for it, me friend, will you be wantin' a fresh plug or one already well chewed like the one you gave me girl?'

Ole replied, 'Just some good snoosh'll be just fine,' but hardly anyone heard him amid the laughter.

Hannah reached a hand over and laid it on Andrew's arm. She squeezed his arm, then left her hand there for a long while.

Not long enough to suit Andrew, but a long while none the less.

CHAPTER 8

'Hannah! Hannah! Come quick! You gotta see this. We gotta hurry, though.'

Hannah clambered out of her family's wagon.

'What is it, Andrew?'

'The cranes!'

'What?'

'The cranes. They're still on the river.'

'What are you talking about?'

'The Platte River is the main stopover for the cranes when they migrate. You won't believe how many there are. We can see the river from the top of that hill. The cranes are everywhere, down on the river. There's gotta be thousands of 'em. C'mon!'

Grabbing her hand he pulled her in the direction he had indicated. She gripped his hand and began to run, suddenly infected by his excitement. Hand in hand they ran up the hill. Just before they reached the top Andrew stopped. He held a finger to his lips.

'Gotta be sorta quiet now. We'll crawl on up to where we can see. I was here a while ago. From on top there we can see the river. You won't believe this.'

Still holding her hand, he began to crawl. She pulled her hand free so she could crawl, mindful that she was probably going to ruin her dress. What would her mother say if she came back with grass stains all over it?

She looked at Andrew as they crawled. Both of them had begun to breathe more normally after the uphill sprint. His face was still animated by his excitement.

Even as they ran, the raucous noise she couldn't identify had puzzled her. Now as they approached the top of the hill, it was almost deafening.

She raised her head enough to look over the hill's crest. She caught her breath. Every square foot of ground along the river, for as far as she could see in both directions, was covered with large, grayish-white birds. Their collective chattering and squawking created the loudest din she could remember hearing.

'There are so many!' she exclaimed.

'Far as you can see,' he agreed.

Just then, as if on some signal, a flock of the birds directly in front of them leaped into the air. Huge wings began beating rhythmically as they rose into the sky. As if it were a signal, every crane in sight in both directions exploded into flight at the same time. The flapping of their wings sounded even louder than had the din of their squawking. Hannah found it impossible to believe that they didn't collide with each other, beat one another with those massive wings, because there were too many, so close together. The sky grew dark as the sheer numbers of the birds blanked out the sun. It seemed as if a giant, dark cloud, emitting as much noise as a cyclone, surrounded them.

Without seeming to be aware she was doing it, she stood up. She flung her arms out to both sides and turned slowly round and round, staring upward at the birds. She felt as she were about to be buried alive by birds. Impulsively she reached her arms around Andrew, hugging him fiercely. Her face was tight against his chest, but remained turned up toward the impossible, endless flock of cranes. She clung to Andrew as if he could protect her from their massive presence. She wanted to hide from them yet at the same time she wanted to open her arms to them, embrace them, become, somehow, one with them. She kept her arms wrapped around Andrew instead.

In moments they were gone. The air grew still. She felt as if something awesome and wonderful had happened. Now it was gone and the world was silent and empty.

She looked up into Andrew's face. She realized abruptly that they were standing with their arms wrapped around each other.

'Oh, Andrew! That was … that was … magnificent. It was beautiful. Thank you for showing me.'

'You're beautiful too,' he responded.

She felt her cheeks redden, but she made no effort to move away from him.

'Where did they all go so suddenly?'

'Out to find stuff to eat. They'll be back at sundown.'

'Oh, I have to see them again. Will we … we won't be able to stay, will we?'

He smiled down at her. 'Won't matter. Frank says they're usually already gone by this time, but it's a late spring. For the next two or three days, the river'll be covered with 'em every night.'

'Then we'll get to see them again?'

'Yup. I'll find us as spot afore dark where we can watch 'em take off again in the mornin', if you want me to.'

'Oh, please do! Can we maybe watch them land on the river tonight? Will we be where we can see?'

'I'm not sure. I'll sure find a spot to show 'em to you if I can.'

'Thank you,' she said again.

It was intended as a simple thanks. Andrew clearly hoped she'd find an unspoken way to express her gratitude. He bent his head down. To his disappointment she turned her head away.

'We better get back,' she said. 'The wagons are already moving.'

'We could catch up later,' he suggested.

She gave him a playful shove and turned away again. As they hurried back to the wagons it seemed perfectly natural that her hand should find his again.

CHAPTER 9

'Hey! You ready?'

Hannah responded instantly. 'Sure. I just finished the chores Mother wanted me to do. Have they come in yet?'

'Not yet. They're due any time, though.'

'I saw men heading over toward the river just a little bit

ago. Where are they all going?'

'They're hiding along the river. They're going to see if they can shoot a bunch of 'em to bolster our meat supply.'

'Are they good eating?'

'Yeah. That's what Frank says, anyway. He says they're way better than geese, even. There's a lot of meat on each one, too. They're big.'

'Oh, I know!' she enthused. 'I can't wait to watch them come in to the river. Do you have a spot picked out?'

'Yeah. I got us a great spot picked. We can lie in a bunch of brush where we have a clear view of the river, but they won't see us, even if they fly right over us.'

Hand in hand, fingers intertwined, they walked quickly toward the hill that separated the circled wagons from the river. Normally they would have camped closer to the water, but they had deliberately left the trail and stayed far enough away to not jeopardize the chance to augment their meat supply.

'Here,' Andrew said, pointing to a clump of brush. 'We can crawl through right here, and be able to see just fine.'

'At least Mother has started letting me wear pants like I always did on the farm at home. I've felt like I had to dress up like it was Sunday every day since we left.'

'Why wouldn't she let you dress like you are now?'

She knew she blushed slightly, but she didn't really care. His eyes wandered down the button-front blouse that accentuated her figure, then tucked into the narrow waist of her trousers. She saw with approval the arousal that her figure inspired in him. He almost forgot where they were or why, so lost was he in staring at her.

It wasn't the first time he had seen her in what she called

her 'work clothes'. Her mother had finally conceded permission to wear them so that she could ride her horse. After long and exhaustive arguments she had convinced both parents that it was only right that she should take a turn herding the livestock along as the wagons pressed westward. It had been a little more of a struggle to persuade them that she needed to be paired with Andrew when she had that duty, because 'she knew she could trust him'.

'Uh, here!' Andrew said as if suddenly waking from a reverie. He pointed to a gap in the brush.

Taking her cue from him, she dropped to hands and knees. Side by side they crawled through the narrow aisle in the brush. Abruptly there was no brush in front of them. Instead the ground dropped steadily all the way to the river. It was so wide!

She said as much. 'The river is so wide. It looks wider than the Missouri.'

'It is, right here. It ain't very deep, though. It's real wide with spring run-off still. But it's always shallow. I think Platte is an Indian word that means "flat water" or something.'

'Could you wade across it?'

'I ain't sure it's that flat. Late in the summer I'd bet you could.'

'Where are all the men?'

'They're hid down there somewhere.'

'Oh.'

'They just don't have anyone so good to wait with.'

Lying side by side, flat on their stomachs, she turned her head toward him. His closeness surprised her. She had scarcely had time to notice what he was about to do when his lips met hers. Her pang of disappointment was mingled with relief as he simply kissed her lightly, then pulled away.

The closeness of her body beside him sent fire coursing through Andrew's whole being. Thoughts of the cranes and their imminent approach faded to some insignificant corner of his mind.

She pulled her head back and looked deeply into his eyes. The unnaturally bright gleam of his gaze told her he was as affected as she. The moment ended abruptly. Without warning the setting sun was blotted from sight. The thunder of thousands of wings swept across the sky above them.

As if suddenly caught in a tryst by angry parents, they jerked apart. Their gaze shot upward. Thousands upon thousands of cranes stopped the beating of their wings and spread them to glide to a landing spot that each bird seemed to have selected.

The sudden ceasing of the beating of all those wings plunged the world into an almost eerie silence. It was abruptly broken by the roar of at least a dozen guns. Birds flailed and tumbled from their landing glide, plummeting to the ground. Seconds later a second volley of fire brought down equal or greater numbers of the majestic creatures.

Cranes who were gliding in to land suddenly began frantically beating their wings, lifting back into the skies. Those who had already landed rose up to join them. As they did, the roar of all those wings mingled with alarmed and angry squawking and screeching. It seemed to Hannah that the fearful clamor would drive her into the ground. She fought against the rising tide of irrational terror. The surging wave of the uproar threatened to carry her away by the force of its intolerable volume.

She clung to Andrew with desperation. Then, suddenly,

the noise was gone, and so were the cranes.

'Where did they go?' she asked.

'Away,' he said with infuriating simplicity.

'Away where?'

He shrugged, suddenly far more interested in her than in the disappearing birds. 'Wherever they find a different spot to land, I guess. They may come back in a little bit. Either that or they'll land down the river a bit, and some others will land here.'

She looked back to the river. 'The men are gathering up the ones they shot. We'll have plenty of meat for a couple days.'

'Yeah,' he said, his voice sounding as if he hadn't really even heard what she said. He reached out a hand and moved a strand of hair back away from her face. 'You are so beautiful,' he breathed.

She rewarded him with a kiss, though neither as long nor as passionate as he obviously wanted.

'It's getting dark,' she observed.

'Yeah.'

'So we better get back.'

'Why? Scared of the dark?' he teased.

'I'm scared of you in the dark, Romeo,' she retorted.

He moved his hand upward from her waist, watching her closely. She took hold of his hand and pushed it gently away.

'Be careful,' she warned. 'We need to go back.'

She began to crawl backward, retracing their path into the brush patch. He followed, reluctantly and disappointed. He tried his best not to show the disappointment. At the edge of the brush they rose and walked, hand in hand, back to the wagons.

Looking around to make sure nobody was watching, he risked the attempt to kiss her goodbye at the edge of her wagon. Instead of shying away she returned the kiss quickly, then climbed the wheel into the wagon. He really appreciated her change of attire as he watched her do so in the gathering darkness.

CHAPTER 10

Four days later they were past where the cranes stopped over during their migration. That was fine with Hannah. She was already tired of a steady diet of crane. Baked crane, fried crane, boiled crane and noodles, boiled crane and dumplings, creamed crane over biscuits, crane hash and crane stew. Crane, two meals a day, day after day. She also knew they had enough meat on hand for at least another couple days.

At least she could share the feeling with Andrew without getting the lecture about being thankful for what God graciously placed in their hands. What time she could slip away and spend with him was absolutely heavenly all by itself.

She surprised herself by wondering, one day, whether people could get married in a wagon train. Some wagon trains were religious groups, like the Mormons, so they would have someone who could perform weddings. Some of the larger wagon trains had a preacher's family included, according to gossip. Theirs was mostly made up of Christians like her and Andrew, but they didn't have a parson in the group.

There was a church at Fort Kearney, she had noticed, but they hadn't been there over a Sunday, so she didn't know what kind of church it was. Was it part of the fort? Was it an Indian mission? If so, was there a Catholic priest heading it up? Would a Catholic priest marry anyone who wasn't Catholic? It didn't matter now. Fort Kearney was behind them.

Maybe it wasn't necessary to find a church. Did the wagon master have the authority to conduct weddings, the way the captain on a ship did? She knew no way to find out without asking. That would release a whole beehive of questions and accusations. She would probably be forbidden to keep seeing Andrew in that case. She would die if that happened!

Was Andrew even that serious about her? Well, he was serious about her. That was for sure. It was getting more and more difficult to maintain control of things when she was with him. He certainly wasn't helping in that regard either.

They forded the South Platte branch of the river without any real problems. Kitty Provost fell out of her family's wagon into the river. She had to be fished out by one of the men on horseback. She was cold and wet, and her parents were as terrified as she was. She had never been in any real danger though, Hannah thought. The Platte wasn't anything like the Missouri.

The next fort they would come to would be Fort Laramie, according to her father. That was still a long way away.

She was sitting beside her mother, half asleep as the wagon rocked and rattled. Movement on the hill ahead and to the left caught her eye. Something was moving there, but it was too far away for her to see what. She pointed at it.

'What's that?' she asked her mother. Her mother did

hardly more than glance at it.

'One of the outriders, I suppose.'

Hannah shrugged her shoulders. She allowed herself to slip into the daydream she had come to resist less and less. It always involved Andrew. Of course. Why wouldn't it? She sighed deeply.

She looked up to see if she could see the outrider any more clearly. It might be him. She didn't know what he was assigned to do today. Since Fort Kearney he had been assigned a full man's portion of the work, so he might be anywhere.

She was surprised that the rider had come so much closer. It was somebody on horseback, leading something. Another animal. It was a packhorse. That wasn't an outrider.

'Mother, that's not an outrider!' she exclaimed.

Her mother looked up, finally giving full attention to what her daughter was saying. Hannah heard a sharp intake of breath from her mother.

'No. It isn't,' Fannie affirmed. 'I'm not sure what it is. I hope Frank or somebody has spotted him.'

Almost immediately Hannah saw another rider, on the other side of the one in question. Even from this distance she recognized Andrew by the way he rode his horse.

'I think that's Andrew behind him,' she informed her mother. 'He must be one of the outriders today, and he's seen him.'

The wagon train did not pause in its progress. It simply continued on its crawling course along the rutted trail. All eyes, however, were by now focused on the unknown person who approached.

As they drew closer together, the man moved off the

trail and sat his horse, simply waiting. He was the strangest looking person Hannah had ever seen.

'Is ... is he a mountain man, Mother?'

Fannie frowned thoughtfully. 'Well, he certainly looks like the descriptions of mountain men that I've heard. But there aren't any mountains for at least another hundred miles. Maybe farther.'

The man was dressed all in buckskins, down to and including the moccasins on his feet. The only thing he wore that didn't fit that description was a well-weathered hat with a broad brim. The shadow from the brim made it difficult to distinguish his features, but it was clear that he had a full beard.

His horse had a hackamore that was braided from something other than leather. Instead of a saddle he had a blanket on the horse's back. It seemed to be of flannel or some such material, but it was so matted with dirt and hair and grime that it was impossible to tell.

The load on the packhorse was secured with ropes that might have been made of rawhide. It was very expertly tied, however, with perfect diamond hitches.

'I wonder what he wants?' Hannah asked her mother.

'I have no idea. More than likely he's just waiting for us to pass.'

'Frank is coming to talk to him, it looks like.'

'I'm sure he has the situation well in hand. You would do better to get back to your embroidery and worry less about passers-by.'

'It's hard to do a nice job on embroidery. The wagon bounces around too much.'

It was especially difficult to do any embroidery when she

kept craning her neck to get a better look at the stranger. As their wagon passed by where he and Frank were sitting their horses and talking, he looked up. His eyes met Hannah's. His eyes were brown, but the palest brown eyes she had ever seen. They seemed to look right through her, or at least deep into her soul. She let out a startled gasp and instantly looked down at the material in her hands.

'What was that about?' her mother demanded.

'I … I have no idea,' Hannah stammered. 'I just didn't expect him to be looking at me like that.'

'Like what?'

'I don't know, Mother. I don't really know.'

In fact, she didn't. She would certainly remember the moment, however.

CHAPTER 11

It was his turn to be an outrider. Andrew relished the fact. He was stationed at left front today. He especially enjoyed being a front rider. It didn't matter which side of the trail he was assigned to.

As an outrider it was his responsibility to maintain a good distance beside and in front of the wagon train. He was the one expected to notice anything of importance ahead of them. That might be almost anything. It could be a herd of buffalo, Indians, or a stretch of difficult trail.

His reaction to anything would be a matter of judgment. If it were Indians, of course, he would try to get an idea of how many and what their intentions might be, then speed back to the wagons to sound the warning.

Once he spotted a small herd of pronghorn antelope. He galloped back to the train and reported it. At Frank's instruction, the two of them and one other man loped back to where he had spotted them. When they again spotted them in the distance, Frank said,

'Put the horses down there in the draw and tie 'em to some brush.'

When they had done so he led them on hands and knees to a large patch of tall brush.

'Get down and lie quiet,' he instructed.

He removed his neckerchief. Pulling the highest branch down, he tied the neckerchief to it, then allowed it to spring upright. He noted the direction the neckerchief blew, fluttering and flapping in the breeze.

'Wind's away from 'em,' he commented 'Just perfect. Just stay still now an' wait.'

'What'd you do that for?' Andrew asked.

'You'll never get close enough to them antelope to get a shot,' Frank explained. 'The only way to get them is get 'em to come to you. They're about the most curious animal there is. By now they've already spotted that thing flappin' in the wind. In half an hour they'll be right over here to check it out, as long as we stay outa sight.'

They all squirmed down into the grass and brush as far as they could. They removed their hats so that they would be less visible. On Frank's orders, they refrained from lifting their heads to see if his tactic was working.

Andrew didn't know how Frank knew when it was time to look. Probably he knew about how long it would take to accomplish the goal from experience. After what had seemed like an interminable amount of time, he whispered,

'OK now. Get your rifles out in front of you. Rise up just enough to see, pick out a big one and shoot it. Aim careful. You ain't apt to get a second shot.'

Acting as one they each rose enough, rifles already to shoulders, to see over the grass. Less than fifty yards away the whole herd of antelope stood, steadfastly staring at the fluttering neckerchief. Three rifles barked almost in unison. Three antelope dropped to the ground.

The rest of the herd wheeled and galloped away, running at incredible speed. Andrew stood, mouth agape, watching.

'Wow!' he breathed. 'Look how fast they run! I didn't know anything could run that fast.'

An hour later they had ridden back to the wagons, each with a dressed-out antelope slung across his saddle. The meat was divided up among the wagons, and later everyone learned what antelope meat tasted like. Not everybody was favorably impressed.

'It tastes funny,' Hannah complained.

'It's a mite gamy all right,' Will agreed. 'Frank says if they've been runnin' afore they're shot it's a whole lot stronger. He said it'd be stronger'n the venison we ate once in a while at home, regardless. He says we'll likely have a chance at a deer now and then. More'n likely we'll get a chance to get a buffalo or two. He says for us not to shoot more'n one at a time, though. They got too much meat for us all to eat afore it commences to spoil.'

'I hope it tastes better than antelope,' Hannah complained again.

Looking for another chance to be the one to discover

some sort of game, Andrew was being especially careful to peer over the top of each hill before he exposed himself. As usual, he had ridden a little more than a mile ahead of the wagons, being sure he scouted far enough ahead to provide advance notice of anything of interest.

He was sure he had spotted the mountain man without being seen. He had just peered over the crest of a hill when he caught a glimpse of him. He ducked instantly. He dismounted, left Buster ground-tied, and crawled to the top of the hill. He picked a spot with a large clump of something Frank had called soap weeds. From its cover he watched the strange-looking man for quite a while.

He didn't appear to be in any hurry to get anyplace. He rode on the trail, heading eastward. Andrew wasn't sure why, but he had the distinct impression that the man was waiting for the wagon train to arrive where he was rather than aiming to get someplace else.

He remounted his horse and paralleled the newcomer, careful to stay behind him and out of sight. Or at least he thought he did. It was difficult for him to ride slowly enough not to overtake the man, though.

As the wagon train came into sight the man moved off to the side of the trail and stopped. The train was still a quarter-mile away when Frank loped out to meet him. As he did so Andrew moved closer to the top of a low rise, where Frank could easily see him.

He was too far away to hear the conversation. He watched until the wagons were past the pair, and the newcomer had fallen in behind the last wagon, clearly joining the group. That fact irritated Andrew, but he had no idea why. Frank waved him back to his post.

CHAPTER 12

'You must be the wagon master.'

'That's me.'

'Glad to meet you. I'm Jeremiah Smith, at your service.'

The newcomer extended a hand, leaning over the side of his horse to reach out as far as he could. Frank responded in kind, returning the strong grip of the other's handshake.

'Headin' for Oregon?' Smith asked.

'Yup.'

'A wee hair late gettin' started, ain't ya?'

'Yeah, a little. We're making pretty good time, though.'

'Any trouble crossin' the south fork o' the Platte?'

'Nope. Went nice an' smooth.'

'That's one advantage o' bein' a mite late. You let the worst o' the spring run-off get past afore you gotta swim it.'

'Where you headin' for?'

The mountain man studied Frank for a moment.

'Well, to be totally honest, I was just sorta amblin' along nice an' slow waitin' for you to get here.'

The answer clearly surprised Frank. A couple of the other men had ridden out to join them. They sat their horses, listening silently.

'Why would you be waitin' for us?'

'Well, I spotted your smoke last evenin', just afore dark. I been hopin' I could catch up with some folks headin' to Oregon.'

'Why Oregon? The trappin' business 'bout petered out?'

Jeremiah sighed. 'Seems thataway. Oh, I can still trap lots o' stuff. There just ain't nothin' to do with 'em after I trap 'em. I brung my furs to where I thought there'd be a ron-dayview, but there wasn't one at all. Oh, there was a couple o' fur buyers there, but not like the old days. The ones that was there wouldn't pay but half what they was worth. Folks is all wantin' silk hats now, they say, so nobody wants beaver no more.'

'You don't wanta go back East, huh?'

'No way! I started out back East. Too many people. Too much gov'ment. Nossir, I figger Oregon, now there's the new land o' opportun'ty. O' course my chances o' gettin' clear to Oregon all by myself is somewhere betwixt slim an' none. So I'm sittin' there starin' into my campfire one evenin', and I says, "Jeremiah, you just needs to find yourself a wagon train headin' to Oregon, an' join up with 'em."'

'Why would a wagon train want you taggin' along?'

'That's just exactly what I asked myself, in the very next breath. So I started thinkin' about it. I know the country plumb good as far as Fort Bridger, an' halfway good on over to Fort Hall. I can talk to at least half the Indians a fella's apt to meet along the way. The ones I can't talk to I can sure palaver with in sign language. I can scout farther an' faster than any white man you got.'

As Frank paused, clearly thinking about it, Smith went on. 'Oh, by the way, that fella you got on the ridge behind me there ain't half bad, for a green scout. I pertneart didn't see 'im when he first spotted me. Just got one little mite of a glimpse afore he ducked back down. If I hadn't got that first glimpse so I knowed he was there, I might not've spotted 'im till halfway betwixt there an' here.'

Frank's eyes darted up to where Andrew sat his horse, watching, then he looked quickly back at Smith. He was clearly impressed. He hadn't noticed the mountain man so much as glance in that direction, but he obviously knew Andrew's position. He would discuss it later with the lad and see if Jeremiah's description of his first glimpse was accurate. It might, in fact, be of value to the group to have such an experienced denizen of the wilderness along. Frank pushed his hat to the back of his head.

'Well, I'd have to have a vote o' the folks afore I could OK anything like that,' he explained. 'We do things democratic-like, except when I have to pull rank for the sake o' the group's safety. In the meantime you can go ahead and drop in behind us an' tag along. You're sure welcome for supper an' the night, either way.'

'Well, now, that sounds as fair as anything could be,' Smith replied. 'It'll be right good to have folks to talk with. I already heard pertneart everything I got to say, an' I'm gettin' a mite bored hearin' me say it all over again.'

He lifted his reins and kicked his horse into motion, falling in behind the last wagon, which had just passed where they sat talking.

CHAPTER 13

Sundays were wonderful! Hannah stretched lazily and sat up in bed. The sun was already up. It was great to have that extra hour's sleep. She dressed quickly and climbed down from the wagon.

The camp was already astir. The big fire was already built

in the center of the wagons' circle. Several of the women were working on preparation of the common meal that would cook in a dozen Dutch ovens in the coals of that fire.

'You folks don't travel on Sundays, I take it?'

The voice at her elbow startled her. She whirled and came face to face with the man who had joined himself to the wagon train the day before. She jumped and took a step backward.

'Oh! You startled me. I didn't hear you walk up.'

'Beggin' your pardon, ma'am. I didn't mean to make you jump like that. The name's Jeremiah Smith.'

He extended a hand. Hesitant, she started to hold out her hand, started to bring it back, then went ahead and reached out and shook hands with him.

'I ... I'm ... I'm Hannah Henford. I ... I'm pleased to meet you.'

'I am pleased to meet you too, Hannah Henford. If I dare say so, you are indeed a welcome sight to a man who's been too much alone for far too long.'

Hannah's mind whirled. He smelled! It wasn't a repugnant smell, though. He smelled of smoke and body oils, and maybe that's just what buckskin smells like. His beard hadn't been combed or trimmed in a very long time. He smelled ... musky. That's what it was. She didn't know where that word came from but it popped into her mind.

He wasn't as old as she'd first thought. His beard had tinges of red in it here and there. His long hair trailed down to his shoulders, thick and ... and ... wild. It looked as if it wanted to curl, but the weight of its length kept it from doing so.

His eyes were brown, but they were that strikingly pale

...that had shocked her when she first saw him. They ...bright, alive, almost laughing at her, she thought.

'Rachel,' he said.

'What?'

'I was tryin' to think of what your name should oughta be. Hannah just doesn't seem to quite fit ya. Then it hit me. You read the Bible, don't ya?'

'What? Yes. Of course. Do ... do you?'

'Betchyer boots I do. Pack it with me. You remember Rachel?'

'She ... she was Jacob's wife.'

'Uh-huh. And she was so beautiful that when Jacob done took one look at 'er, he offered to work for her pa for seven years if he could just have her. An' he did the work. Then her ol' man done cheated him an' palmed off the ugly daughter on 'im instead, but Rachel was so beautiful he went an' worked another seven years so he could have her. Now that's one beautiful woman.'

'I ... always felt sorry for Leah,' Hannah offered. 'She was Jacob's wife, but Jacob didn't want her. But he couldn't back out of the deal after he'd ... uh ... married her.'

'That's a fact. Then he struck up that deal with his father-in-law and got Rachel too, for workin' another seven years.'

'Yes, but he got to marry Rachel before he worked the other seven years. He got to marry her just one week after he'd married Leah.'

'So he got to marry Rachel after all.'

Hannah nodded, a shadow of melancholy darkening her eyes.

'So then poor Leah just got shunted off to one side and almost ignored. She even had to bargain with Rachel whenever she wanted to … to sleep with her husband.'

'Plumb raw deal, wasn't it?'

'It sure seems like it.'

'But that Rachel must have been one beautiful woman. That's why I think your name shoulda been Rachel.'

'My … my name's Hannah. It's Biblical too.'

'Oh, I am familiar with that name also. A fine Godly woman she was, too. And loved by her husband Elkanah, they ain't no doubt. But Rachel, now there was a woman whose beauty was special. It was over an' above just beautiful, it was.'

'I … I really need to get going. My mother is going to be needing some help.'

He took off his worn hat – she wasn't at all sure what color it had originally been – swept it out beside himself as he offered her a deep bow.

'Then by all means, you should go … Rachel.'

Furious at herself because she was sure she was blushing, she whirled and hurried to where her mother and the other women busied themselves. All the way there she felt his eyes on her back. When she was almost there she chanced a quick peek over her shoulder. Sure enough he was there, leaning against the front corner of their wagon, rifle tilted against him, arms folded, just watching her.

She did her best to ignore him, plunging into the peeling of the potatoes her mother was working on. Fannie looked at her closely. She looked back at their wagon. The mountain man was just disappearing around the wagon, heading toward a small cluster of men who were talking.

'Is anything wrong?' she asked her daughter.

Hannah felt her face flame again. 'No. Nothing's wrong.'

'You seem flustered.'

'Oh, I … I … It's nothing. I was just caught off guard a little.'

'By what? Or should I say, by whom?'

Hannah looked at her mother sharply, then dropped her gaze.

'It was just that man who joined the wagon train yesterday. He … just sort of frightened me.'

'Whatever did he do to scare you?'

'Nothing, really. I just hadn't seen him, and he spoke to me and I turned around and he was just … so close. It startled me.'

'Did he say anything?'

'Yes. We talked for a couple minutes. It seems strange, but Mother, he knows how to read.'

'Why wouldn't he?'

'Well, I don't know. I just thought mountain men had always been in the wilderness, living like … like savages.'

Her mother laughed. 'No, dear. Most of them became mountain men because they like being alone, or because they wanted to make a great deal of money in a short time by trapping, or because they were running from something. Some of them are from very famous families back East.'

'Really?'

'Really.'

'Then it's not strange that he … reads the Bible?'

'He reads the Bible?'

'He said so. He says he always has his Bible with him. He knew who Hannah was in the Bible, and even her husband's name, and he knew about Jacob and … and Rachel.'

As she said the last name she was afraid she was blushing

again. She concentrated on the potato in her hands to hide the fact.

'You must have talked with him quite a while,' her mother ventured.

Hannah shook her head more vigorously than the comment should have required.

'No. No, just for a couple minutes. I told him I needed to get over here and help you.'

Fannie studied her as they worked for a few minutes, then she said,

'I thought you and Andrew were going for a walk this morning.'

'Oh!' Hannah said, her head jerking up. 'That's what I was getting ready to do when I … when he … when … when I started talking to … to him.'

'And you got so flustered you forgot you were going for a walk with Andrew?'

Face flaming, Hannah sputtered and struggled to explain what she couldn't explain, even to herself. Her mother finally rescued her.

'You don't really need to help here, Hannah. Why don't you go ahead and go for your walk.'

Hannah dropped the potato she had halfway peeled. Wiping her hands in her apron she looked around. The mountain man was busily engrossed in conversation with three other men. Trying to get a wagon or two between herself and the group she walked swiftly toward the Stevensons' wagon. Andrew was already waiting,

'Hi!' he greeted, his eyes saying far more than his words.

Still flustered, Hannah said, 'I'm sorry I'm late. I … got sidetracked for a little bit.'

'Your folks didn't want you to go walkin' with me?'

'Oh, no. It's not that. I asked Mother last night if it was all right if we went for a walk today.'

'Good. I don't really wanta face your pa if he thinks you're sneakin' off with me.'

She didn't answer, content for them to walk side by side. He led her on a path directly away from the circle of wagons, moving toward the river but upriver from where they were camped. As always, they had camped nearly a quarter-mile away from the river itself. That provided closer proximity of adequate grazing for the livestock, and a less cluttered place to camp. It was amazing the things previous wagon trains had cast aside, just leaving their cast-offs lying on the prairie. Some of the most popular camping sites were almost like garbage dumps. It disgusted her.

As soon as he was sure they were well out of sight of everyone in the camp he reached out and took hold of her hand. She responded, intertwining their fingers together, letting their connected arms swing back and forth, following the rhythm of their steps. And of her heart. She turned her head so she could look at him, staring into his eyes.

'Oh, Andrew, I feel so safe when I'm with you.'

'I think I love you, Hannah Leigh Henford,' he breathed.

'I … I think I love you too,' she responded. She might have said more, but his lips made it impossible for her to do so. She didn't mind. The kiss was long, lingering.

Once again it was Hannah who drew back. Her mind was saying, *We better slow down!* while her emotions were saying, *I want more!*

'Do you have someplace in mind to walk?' she asked, feeling breathless.

'Yeah. C'mon.' he took her hand, entwining his fingers again with hers. She followed his lead for quite a long way until they came out on a gentle hill that sloped down toward the river.

Along the river great cottonwoods, elm, oak and ash trees provided a ribbon of hardwood forest in an otherwise almost treeless plain. The cottonwoods dominated. They were in 'cotton phase'. Their seeds, each encased in a fluffy sphere of white gossamer fibers, appeared something like small, weightless bolls of cotton. Every slightest breeze dislodged countless numbers of them from the trees. They floated on the breeze, filling the air with the 'cotton' until they looked like huge unseasonal snowflakes. They hung so thickly in the air Hannah would occasionally inhale one into her nose, being forced to blow it out quickly, then, often, sneeze.

A profusion of wild flowers presented a riot of brilliant colors. At the edge of the trees, chokecherry and wild-plum bushes were in full bloom.

'Oh, Andrew, it's so beautiful.'

'So are you, Hannah Leigh,' he said, staring deeply into her eyes.

They kissed again, long, lingeringly, reveling in the emotions that surged within them.

He sat down suddenly, pulling her down beside him. She sat down, brought her feet in close to her and hugged her knees.

'It just looks like paradise, doesn't it?'

'When I'm with you, anything's paradise,' he said.

'If anything's really paradise any more,' she responded wistfully. A mischievous gleam sparked in his eyes.

'It would all be paradise if it wasn't for a woman, you know.'

She whirled on him with pretended wrath.

'Andrew Stevenson, first you say I make your world a paradise then you say if it wasn't for me it would be paradise. You're terrible!'

She loomed over him and began to tickle him in the ribs on both sides. He responded by grabbing her by the waist and turning her over so he was on top, tickling her in the same manner.

They tussled and rolled together in the deep grass and wild flowers, laughing and struggling for advantage. As he once again rolled so he was on top he stopped. Their faces were inches apart. They didn't remain that way. Immediately they were locked in another increasingly passionate kiss.

Andrew glanced down. In the course of their tumbling over and over her dress had pulled up far enough for her knee to be clearly visible. She wasn't wearing the long bloomers he thought were standard for a woman wearing a dress.

His hand darted down onto the bared knee. She squirmed and pushed his hand away. With a free hand she pulled at her dress to cover more of her legs. Even as she did so, the other hand maintained its position around his shoulders, holding him where he was.

'Andrew,' she breathed, 'behave yourself. We don't want to … to … go that far.'

'I do,' he argued instantly.

'Mmm. That much is obvious. But I'm not that kind of girl.'

'But I love you, Hannah Leigh.'

'I love you too, Andrew Clyde Stevenson. More than I

have ever loved anyone. But we need to wait.'

'What is it we're waiting for?' he demanded. 'We already know we love each other.'

'You know what we're waiting for,' she insisted. 'Nobody wants to buy the cow if the milk's free. And this milk isn't free, my darling.'

He leaned forward and kissed her again. 'So let's get married.'

Staying there, their faces mere inches apart, she asked,

'And just how would you plan to go about that?' she brushed his hair away from the side of his face affectionately.

That was clearly beyond where his mind had been thinking and planning.

'I ... I don't know. I bet we can manage it, though, if we think about it.'

She sat up straighter and twisted herself so that she was facing somewhat away from him. She leaned against him. They sat there together, he in frustrated disappointment, she with torn emotions. She snuggled against him, filling her eyes with nature's beauty spread out before them.

'Oh, look!' she said.

On the far side of the river a doe with a spotted fawn at her side stepped into the edge of the water. She drank deeply. Mimicking its mother's action, the fawn stuck his nose in the water, then jerked back. He shook his head. A minute later he tried it again, with the same result.

One of the watchers must have moved. The doe's head jerked up. She sniffed the air. She nuzzled the fawn away from the water and began to walk swiftly away from the open area. They disappeared in thick brush. Scarcely a minute later she emerged from the brush and hurried away alone.

'Where's her baby?'

'She hid it. It'll be lyin' in that brush somewhere. They hide so good you can walk right past 'em and not know they're there. They ain't got no scent yet, so even a coyote or a wolf or somethin' can walk right by 'em and not spot 'em.'

'Will she come back?'

'Oh sure. Probably about dark. She'll come back an' get it an' let it suck 'cause it'll be hungry, then they'll go off somewheres.'

'That is so beautiful,' she breathed.

'So are you,' he said. 'Can I be your hungry fawn?'

She elbowed him in the ribs, laughing. He stifled her laugh with his lips.

To his further disappointment she kissed him quickly and turned her head back to continue watching the river. After a moment of silence she said,

'Did you know that mountain man can read?'

'What?'

'The mountain man. The guy that joined our wagon train. Did you know he can read?'

'No. How would I know that? How do you know that?'

'He told me.'

'So what? Who wants to talk about him anyway? I wanta talk about us.'

She ignored the comment. 'He said he reads his Bible all the time. He always has it with him.'

His irritation was written eloquently all over his face. 'Why would he be tellin' you somethin' like that?'

An impish grin played at the corners of her mouth. 'He told me I should be named Rachel instead of Hannah.'

'What? Why?'

'Because he says Rachel must have been the most beautiful woman ever, for Jacob to work for her father for that long just to get to marry her.'

'When were you talking to him, anyway?'

'This morning. He was right by the wagon when I got up.'

Andrew's mood changed abruptly. She wasn't sure whether it was anger or jealousy that so tightly accentuated the lines in his face.

'Why was he right at your wagon when you were gettin' dressed?'

Surprised at this response, she said, 'I don't know that he'd even been there that long. He couldn't have seen anything from there anyway, even if he was. When I got out of the wagon I almost bumped right into him. I think he was just on the way by.'

'And you just happened to have a long conversation about … about all kinds o' stuff that ain't none of his business anyway.'

'Andrew! I was just being polite. He introduced himself, and we shook hands. We just made small talk for a couple minutes, and then we both went on our way.'

Clearly less than satisfied, Andrew insisted, 'It ain't a good idea for you to be talkin' to people like that. We don't really know a thing about 'im.'

'Don't be angry. I was just being polite.'

Andrew tried valiantly to stifle the pangs of fear and jealousy that surged irrationally in him. He was only mildly successful. In any case, the mood of the morning was broken. They walked back to the camp hand in hand, and made no effort to let loose when they were in sight of the others. That, at least, gave Andrew a feeling of satisfaction.

She was willing to 'announce' their relationship to the rest of the group.

Even so, he was not a happy camper the rest of the day.

CHAPTER 14

When Andrew and Hannah rejoined the camp, everyone was gathered at the central fire.

They were all following their Sunday ritual of singing hymns to the accompaniment of Pat's fiddle and Ole's squeeze-box. Pat, who, in light of being the fiddle player, seemed to be in charge, announced they'd sing one more hymn after someone shared something from the Bible, then they'd eat. Just as the hymn ended, Jeremiah Smith spoke up.

'Could I offer to be the one to read a passage or so outa the Good Book afore we eat?'

The question stunned the group, coming as it did from the least expected source. They all stared at him, at a loss how to respond.

'I got my Bible here,' he offered. 'I'd be plumb happy to do the honors.'

Almost every person in the group exchanged looks that hovered between incredulity and shame that none of them had thought to do a reading.

'Sure and 'twould be a fine thing, I'm thinkin',' Pat rushed out the words, recovering from his initial shock. 'You just go right ahead an' read a mite.'

Smith picked up a buckskin package he had laid on the

ground beside him. He untied the strings that held it shut and pulled out a black, leather-bound Bible. He opened it with an obvious familiarity. He read the story of Jacob and Rachel, reading as fluently as a schoolteacher might. Hannah was both surprised and puzzled at the difference between the perfect diction when he read and the casual, uneducated sound of his normal conversation. She was even more nonplussed by the fact that as he read about Jacob and Rachel he kept glancing frequently at her.

Her face flamed red as she realized the reason for the selection. Neither was it lost on Andrew. Even though they were sitting tightly against each other, he felt the need to slip an arm around her waist possessively.

When he had concluded the passage Smith closed his Bible, put it carefully back in the buckskin and laid it aside. Pat began playing another hymn. They all quickly joined in. The meal that followed was as festive and extravagant as always. It was augmented by a wild turkey and a prairie hen the mountain man had brought into camp. Nobody had noticed him leave to hunt for game, nor seen him return. He simply made a comment about wanting to pull his own weight as he laid them on the ground where the fire was being built.

After the meal the singing took its usual course, turning to well-known and popular songs instead of hymns. When it became lively enough to spur people to dance, several couples began to do so. Andrew was just standing up to ask Hannah to dance with him when Smith appeared in front of them.

'Might I have the distinguished pleasure of a dance with Rachel? I mean with Miss Hannah?' he asked.

Hannah shot a glance at Andrew, whose face instantly became suffused with an angry red. She looked at Smith, then back again at Andrew. She wanted to summarily refuse. At the same time she wanted to dance with this untamed denizen of the wilderness. There was also just the matter of custom. He had properly asked her to dance.

'Well, uh … I … I suppose so,' she said.

He instantly grabbed her and whirled her away, dancing with an agility and skill that seemed totally at odds with his persona. Andrew watched, seething with helpless rage.

As soon as the dance was finished he quickly grabbed Hannah for the next dance. The fact that he was neither as light on his feet nor as accomplished as the mountain man did not help him feel any better. None the less he maneuvered to make sure Smith did not have an opportunity to ask Hannah for a repeat dance.

When the dancing stopped and folks sat down, quiet conversations sprang up easily.

'Sure an' I'm bettin' you've got some fine stories to tell was ye a mind to share one or two,' Pat Callahan observed.

'I have in fact had my share of adventures and narrow escapes,' Smith replied. 'As a matter o' fact, one time up along the Yellowstone River I was lookin' for a good spot to set up a trap line when a bunch o' Hunkpapas came ridin' over the hill. There was more'n a dozen of 'em, an' they caught me plumb flat-footed. I knew good an' well they weren't gonna take kindly to my bein' in their territory.' He looked around, assuring himself he had everybody's undivided attention.

'I jumped on my horse and took off, runnin' through the timber. They spotted me right off, o' course, and set after me, a-yellin' an' a-hollerin'.

'They was gettin' uncomfortable close when I decided I couldn't outrun 'em so I'd better think o' somethin' mighty fast. When my horse run under a big ol' pine tree I reached up and grabbed a branch. I gave the horse a good kick as he run out from under me. He was already scared, 'cause he'd smelled them Indians, so he didn't even slow down.

'I climbed up the tree just as fast as I could climb, and hugged the trunk of it nice and tight just as them Hunkpapas came into sight. They went right straight underneath me, never thinkin' to look up, since my horse's tracks just kept right on a-goin'.'

Everyone watched and waited, almost afraid to breathe. Finally someone said,

'Then what did you do?'

'Well, a man on foot is just about as good as dead in that country. I had to get my horse back, that's all there was to it. I climbed back down the tree an' set off after 'em on a run. It didn't take too awful long to catch up to 'em, 'cause without me a-kickin' 'im my horse slowed down enough so's they could catch 'im. I just hid an' watched. They was far enough away I couldn't hear all o' what they was sayin', but they was arguin'. Some of 'em wanted to backtrack to try to find me. The rest just wanted to take the horse and be one horse ahead.'

'You could understand 'em?'

'Oh, sure. Hunkpapa's an awful lot like Lakota, so it ain't hard to understand.'

'How many Indian languages can you speak?'

'Oh, half a dozen or so. Lakota, Shoshone, Arapaho are the ones I'm best at. But I can make out with quite a bunch of others,'cause they're some alike.'

Silence waited while the group waited for him to continue the story. When he didn't, someone asked,

'So what did you do?'

'Well, they decided to just take the horse instead o' lookin' for me, so I just tagged along, keepin' outa sight an' all. When they camped for the night they just left one guy to keep watch o' the horses. I slipped in right after the moon went down, clapped a hand over his mouth and stuck 'im with my knife. Then I took the hobbles off all their horses but one that I thought'd make a good packhorse. I got my rifle an' pack o' stuff back from where they'd piled everything, an' just rode off real quiet like. By the time they woke up the next mornin' their horses would've all wandered off, so they'd be afoot an' one man short. If they did manage to catch their horses again it'd take 'em days. But I decided maybe as how I'd oughta find a different spot for my trapline.'

Once again silence reigned for a long moment. Someone finally ventured,

'Do you think they ever figured out who did it?'

'Oh, I hope so,' he enthused. 'I done told the story around enough to let 'em know they hadn't oughta mess with Jeremiah Smith.'

'Didn't it bother you that you'd killed in cold blood the one watching the horses?'

'Nary a bit,' Smith replied instantly. 'It's an understood thing. They'd already made it plain they was after my hide. It was me or them. Kill or be killed. Now if'n I'da slipped around where the rest of 'em was sleepin', an' slit their throats one at a time, like that fella called Death Wind used to do, then that'd be a different matter. He'd always leave just one alive to wake up an' find everyone else dead as a doornail. The Indians got so's if they heard the wind makin' a certain sound in the trees they'd take it as a omen Death Wind was comin', an' they'd light out, ridin' day an' night to get outa the area.'

'Why would he do that? This Death Wind, I mean,' someone asked.

'Just hated Indians. Indians had killed his family, an' he spent his whole life gettin' even, killin' all the Indians he could.'

'But that's just cold-blooded murder.'

'It sure 'nough is. That's what I said. I don't feel no guilt for killin' the guy watchin' the horses. That's the only way I could survive. My life or his. But I don't go killin' anyone I don't need to. Sorta like David in the Bible. He killed a good many men, but God called him a man after his own heart.'

He continued to regale the group with story after story, each with enough ring of truth to suggest that they just might have happened, but far enough on the edge of credibility to leave some listeners with doubt.

Andrew was certain none of it was true. He eventually got up and walked away, finding something else to do. Hannah looked after him, at a loss to understand his attitude, but too entranced by the mountain man's stories to follow him.

CHAPTER 15

'Hey, beautiful Rachel, have you ever seen a family o' turkeys?'

Hannah looked up. 'My name is Hannah,' she corrected, feigning more anger than she felt.

He chuckled. 'You didn't answer the question.'

'What was the question again?' she asked, though she knew perfectly well.

'I asked if beautiful Rachel would like to see a family of turkeys? It ain't often you get to see a turkey hen with a brood o' babies.'

'Maybe you should ask that person named Rachel about it instead of asking me,' Hannah replied with an impish grin. He grinned in response.

'Well, then, would beautiful Hannah whose name should be Rachel like to watch a hen turkey with her brood?'

'Where?'

'Just over that hill. It ain't far, if they're still there. We can catch up to the wagons in no time.'

She looked around, as if she shouldn't be seen talking with this strange man. She wanted to, though. He fascinated her. She felt some sort of attraction every time she was close to him. The earthy, unwashed, musky smell of him, instead of repulsing her had some strange, almost hypnotic attraction, drawing her to him at the same time as it repelled her. She didn't understand it, but it excited her.

'OK,' she replied.

'C'mon, then,' he said. 'They don't stay in one place for long.'

Almost running to match his long strides she followed him going at right angles to the trail the wagons were following. Over the top of a rise he led her down across a shallow valley and up the other side. Near the top he held a finger to his lips, then dropped to all fours. She followed his example.

They quietly crawled up the side of the hill. Just at the crest he motioned her to get lower. On their stomachs they slithered the last few feet. Silently he pointed.

Across another shallow dip between hills, a large hen turkey was pecking at tender shoots of some sort of weed as she walked. Behind her, strung out in single file, five turkey chicks followed.

As they watched one of the chicks stumbled over something and fell on its nose. It struggled back to its feet and shook its head as if annoyed. Hannah stifled a giggle that threatened to betray their presence.

Just a few feet further on a different chick did the same thing. It got back to its feet and waddled after the others, reforming the perfect single-file line.

They lay there in the grass until the tiny flock had moved over the top of the next rise.

'Oh, that was absolutely darling!' Hannah enthused. 'However did you find them without scaring them?'

He turned over on his side, put his elbow on the ground and cradled his head on his hand.

'I'm a mountain man, beautiful Hannah that should be named Rachel. A mountain man always has to walk soft an' keep 'is eyes open. I spotted 'em one hollow back, an' saw what direction they was goin'. I thought o' you right off, bettin' you hadn't never seen nothin' like that. Them turkey mommas is as alert as any livin' critter, an' it takes a special man to sneak up on 'em. I ran all the way to where you was so we could get here in time to watch 'em.'

She reached out a hand and laid it on his arm.

'That was so sweet of you! Thank you.'

'I am a sweet sort of a fella, for a mountain man, I'll

t. Now don't you think all that effort and concern ghta be worth a small kiss?'

She gave him a playful shove and rose to her feet.

'Those are not for sale, Mr Mountain Man.'

'Then what's a man gotta do to earn such a blessing?'

She ignored the question because she wasn't sure how to answer it. Instead she said,

'We'd better be catching up to the rest. The wagons will be quite a ways ahead of us by now.'

With an exaggerated show of reluctance he rose to his feet and set off. Once again she had to almost run to keep up with him. It was the better part of an hour before they overtook the lumbering wagons. As they neared her wagon she laid a hand on his arm.

'Thank you again. That was really exciting. I'm glad you thought to show them to me.'

He swept off his hat and offered her an exaggerated bow. Grinning he turned and strode away. Hannah watched him, wrestling with the conflicting feelings struggling with each other within her.

CHAPTER 16

'How far ahead of us?'

'Two days, maybe three.'

'That's a long way for a scout to be goin'.'

Jeremiah met Frank's gaze squarely without flinching.

'I ain't lived this long alone without knowin' what's ahead

o' me,' he said. 'We're getting' close to where the Arapahos genr'ly travel comin' north from where they winter.'

'If they're on the move they shouldn't be a problem.'

'They're on the move but they're still some south of us. We'll get close enough for their scouts to spot us, for sure. Not to mention they know there's a lot o' activity on this trail all summer.'

'The Arapaho aren't usually that much of a problem on the trail.'

'I 'llow that all right enough. It's been a tough winter, though. All the tribes that winter down along the east slope've had a tough time of it. They're still a ways from where they're gonna start runnin' onto buffalo. They're likely to think our livestock looks awful invitin'.'

Frank pondered for a long moment. He took a deep breath.

'Well, I guess about all we can do is what we're doin'. We'll double the watch on the livestock at night, as well as the sentries on the camp.'

'Might be safer to offer 'em a few head o' cattle. Enough to feed 'em till they get to the buffalo.'

Frank shook his head. 'I know some of the trains do that. Especially in areas where the danger is highest. I've never been in favor of it. There's game enough out there. Our outriders, as well as you, have been bringin' in game 'most every day. They gotta be able to do the same.'

'One deer or one antelope don't go far with thirty lodges o' women an' kids.'

'It's that big a bunch?'

'That's my guess. I didn't get close enough to get an actual count. Just judgin' by the smoke an' such. I'm guessin' they'll likely stay put about where they are a couple more days. They sent out huntin' parties. If they're lucky, they'll have to have time to take care o' the meat afore they load up an' head north again.'

'Well, if there are that many of them, then I'm sure it's the right decision to refuse any offer of bribery. And that's what it is, in my thinkin'. No, we'll just keep movin' an' keep our eyes peeled.'

Later he called Andrew aside. 'Young man, I need you to do a scouting job.'

Andrew's heart swelled. He knew his diligence and aptitude had been noted by the wagon master, but he hadn't expected this.

'Whatever you need,' he said.

'Smith says there's a large bunch of Arapaho moving north, quite a ways ahead of us and a ways south. He says there are about thirty lodges, which is a pretty big bunch. Something about it just doesn't ring quite true. I'd like for you to ride that direction and see if you can spot 'em without bein' seen. Stick to the low ground between hills just as much as you possibly can. Don't show yourself on top of any hill or ridge if you can help it. When you have to cross a high point, try to do it in timber or brush or something, so you never show yourself on the skyline. When you find somethin' hightail it back here an' let me know.'

'You want me to leave right now?'

'I think I'd like for you to wait until about time for the moon to come up. I'll try to keep Smith occupied at the other side of the wagons. I'd just as soon he didn't see you leave.'

Andrew clearly had something else on his mind, but he

wasn't sure he should ask. Frank noticed anyway.

'Somethin' botherin' you?'

Andrew shook his head. 'Not really. I just wondered if it'd be all right for me to let Hannah know. She might say something to give me away if she doesn't see me.'

'That serious with you two, is it?'

'Yessir.'

Frank mulled it over briefly.

'No, I'd rather you didn't say anything. If she asks, I'll make up somethin' to tell 'er that I sent you off to do.'

It was still an hour from moonrise when Andrew rode quietly away from the camp, heading due south. Half a mile from the wagons he swung due west. Progress was slow for a while. He let his horse pick his way in the darkness. Once the moon came up he nudged the horse to a trot, then to a lope.

He rode all night. After the first couple of miles he slowed the horse to a swift, ground-eating trot. By sunup he was ten miles ahead of the wagon train. He was just about to cross the top of a low ridge when a strange sound caused him to jerk on the reins. He sat stock still, listening.

Whatever the sound had been, it didn't come again. As he sat there, though, he caught a wisp of smoke against the sky directly ahead of him. He frowned. He dismounted and stood at his horse's head, watching.

Within minutes several small columns of smoke began to ascend from nearly the same spot. He frowned. Every instinct told him it was an encampment of some kind, just coming to life for the day. He was too far south for it to be a wagon train on the trail. He wasn't even halfway to where Frank had told him to expect to find the Indians Smith had warned about. No further than he had ridden, the wagon train would be past them in another day. Then the Indians would be behind them. If they chose to attack they would be coming from the direction opposite to that from which they were expected.

He had to know for sure. He led his horse back down into the bottom of the swale and remounted. He nudged the horse forward, following a shallow, broad-bottomed ravine. He guessed it might reach all the way to the river, but it appeared as if it might lead somewhat westward as well.

He kept a careful eye on the sky. Long before he expected to do so, he found himself just one ridge away from the encampment, judging by the smoke.

He dismounted and tied his horse in a copse of small trees at the bottom of the draw. Afoot, he approached the top of the hill. As he neared the crest he removed his hat and dropped to all fours. Nearer the top he lay down and crawled until he was able to see through the grass.

He counted seventeen tepees in an encampment instead of thirty. That was still quite a few Indians. They appeared to be in no hurry to go anywhere, milling about, chatting with one another. The women were busy at cook fires.

In the distance beyond the village he spotted fifteen or twenty horses. It was a long way, but from where he lay it looked as if several children were keeping them together.

He couldn't think of anything further he might learn from where he was. He wasn't about to try to sneak any closer. Right now they would have to look directly into the rising sun to see him. Soon they would have a better chance of spotting him.

He backed off the ridge swiftly, staying lower than he

thought he needed to, just to be safe. When he was sure he was below the line of sight from the village he stood and ran to his horse. He jerked the reins loose from where he had tethered the animal and leaped into the saddle.

He resisted the urge to kick the horse into a run lest he make enough noise to be heard. He was so frightened he was shaking. Half a mile later he threw caution to the winds and kicked the animal into a run.

When the horse's gait began to labor, better sense overcame his fear. He had already ridden the animal all night. He couldn't afford to cause him to give out before he had regained the wagon train. Reluctantly he reined him back to a trot, hoping he would be able to keep up that pace the rest of the way.

It was early afternoon when he heard the first sounds from the wagons. He was amazed how much noise they made to someone away from them, where everything else was quiet.

Very much aware of Frank's desire to keep the mountain man from knowing of his mission, he rode to a point well ahead of the wagon train's location. He crossed over the trail and rode a quarter-mile, then circled to approach about where he thought the livestock should be. He guessed it almost exactly.

He spotted Billy Mosely sitting his horse, watching the herd. He rode up to him, waving as he approached.

'Hey, Andy,' Billy greeted him. 'Where you been?'

Andrew wasn't sure whether it was all right to share where he had been with anyone. He decided caution was the better option.

'Oh, over by the river. I thought I'd look things over,

since we can't usually see the river from the trail.'

'Your horse looks plumb tuckered out, for just goin' that far.'

'Yeah, he was feelin' frisky so I let 'im run a ways. By the time we'd run back again he decided he didn't wanta be that frisky.'

'Yeah, he sure don't look frisky at all now.'

'I gotta go. See you later, Billy.'

'See ya,' Billy responded, frowning at Andrew's back, still less than convinced but having no idea why he should doubt Andrew's story.

Frank had already spotted him in spite of his coming in from the wrong direction. He met him just behind the last of the wagons.

'You're back quicker'n I thought you'd be.'

'I didn't have to ride near as far as we thought I would.'

'That so?'

'Yeah. If it's the same bunch, there's seventeen tepees, not thirty. And they're less'n ten miles ahead of us, almost five miles south o' the trail.'

Frank stared at him as if he wanted to doubt his word.

'You manage to keep from bein' seen?'

'Yeah, I'm sure I did. I likely wouldn't have, but I caught a glimpse o' smoke just as they were startin' their mornin' fires. I sure wasn't expectin' to run onto 'em that quick.'

Frank frowned, looking at nothing for a long moment.

'Now why would we be told they was way ahead of us, when they're that close. We'll be goin' right on past 'em today or tomorrow. They're gonna come around behind us, just as sure's sin,' he muttered.

'That's what I thought, too. If we have all the sentries an' stuff out the other way, they can just ride into the middle of us before we even know they're there.'

'But that'd mean that Smith is a set-up. That'd mean he'd be in it with the Indians.'

That thought hadn't occurred to Andrew. He gaped at the wagon boss.

'You really think so?'

Frank's frown hadn't softened. His lips were drawn to a thin line.

'I'd hate to think a man'd be that two-faced, but it's been done afore. Well, I'll take care of it. You get that horse seen to. He looks pretty jaded. Get yourself some rest too.'

He wheeled and walked away. Andrew hurried to rub his horse down, give him a generous measure of oats, and turn him out with the other livestock. Then he would go in search of Hannah.

CHAPTER 17

'If you'd like, I'd be happy to show you a patch o' mushrooms that'd sure make your ma happy to put in her cookin'.'

Hannah looked at Jeremiah Smith. Somewhere deep within her alarms sounded. She ignored them. He had been a perfect gentleman every time he had made occasion to be alone with her. There had been several such.

That he had deliberately made those occasions she was certain. He was obviously as attracted to her as she had to admit she was to him. He was so different from anyone she had ever known.

At first, his unkempt appearance and the readily evident fact that his buckskins had never experienced soap and water had appalled her. As she grew used to him, however, even the odor that emanated from him had an almost exciting tang. It wasn't body odor, as if he never washed. She had been around people who didn't, and it was a totally different smell. It was abhorrent.

This smell was different from that. It was a mixture of pine, juniper and sage, smoke and animals, with a musky undertone that just made her feel strange when he was close.

'Are you sure they're the safe ones to eat?' she asked.

He laughed. It was the first time she had heard his laughter. She liked it. It had the same sort of feeling that the man himself did. Free. Unrestrained.

'I'da been dead a hundred times over if I didn't know the difference,' he assured her. 'These kind have a fine flavor.'

'Do I need a basket or something?'

He shrugged. 'If you want, I s'pose. You could just as well pile 'em in your apron an' carry 'em thataway.'

She really wanted to let Andrew know where she was going. Or her mother. At the same time, she really didn't want Andrew to know where she was going. Or her mother either, she had to admit.

She had looked for Andrew a while ago, but he didn't seem to be in the camp. Well, it would take quite a while to get the mushrooms and then catch up to the wagons, so she didn't have time to look for him. Besides, she was really excited to be going there with Jeremiah instead of Andrew. He was so much more ... well ... exciting.

It seemed like an awfully long way. She worried they were getting too far away from the wagon train. She very much didn't want him to sense that fear, though. She was a grown woman, after all, and quite capable of taking care of herself.

The mushroom patch was exactly as he had described it. It took only about fifteen minutes for them to gather enough to tax the ability of her apron to hold them. Her mother would be delighted. There would be enough to share with everyone in the wagon train as well. Fresh mushrooms, after all, didn't keep for very long.

Instead of heading back he walked over to a grassy spot and sat down.

'Why don't you just put 'em in a pile there an' come sit beside me a spell. We ain't had as much time to talk as I'd like. A man like me gets plumb lonesome for someone to talk to.'

Once again alarms rang in her mind, but softer, more distant. Certainly not urgently enough to dictate her actions. She dumped the mushrooms carefully in a pile and moved over to sit beside him. She was glad she had chosen to wear the trousers and blouse today. She had considered riding out to be with Andrew for a while if she had some free time, so she had dressed accordingly.

They chatted a few minutes about her family and what they planned when they got to Oregon. He reached up and moved the hair on the near side of her face back over her shoulder. His finger traced the line of her jaw back to her chin. The touch sent little thrills coursing through her.

She wondered what her friends back in Ohio would think if they knew she was alone out in the middle of nowhere with a wild, untamed mountain man. Would they be scandalized or jealous? She found it hard to believe that such a man as this actually found her interesting. No. More than interesting. He was genuinely attracted to her. Not only was it evident, but he had said so more than once.

He suddenly reached a hand around her shoulders and pulled her over to himself. He lowered his face to just inches from her own. He looked into her eyes. She felt almost entranced. He was about to kiss her! And she was about to let him! She suddenly admitted to herself that was exactly what she had hoped for when he invited her to go mushroom hunting.

Their lips met as if it were the most natural thing in the world. He kissed her lightly, then a little more firmly. Then he kissed her with the fire and passion she had expected from him.

She had been more afraid of his breath than the fact that he might kiss her. The concern was swept away by the rising tide of her passion. He backed away for the barest minute, then their lips met again.

His breath was surprisingly sweet. Some part of her mind wondered at the faint flavor. Then she recognized it. Sage! He had chewed some sage leaves, just to have nice breath for her. He had planned for this to be far more than just gathering mushrooms. The realization sent shivers of apprehension through her.

His hand was sliding across her shoulder, starting down the front of her blouse. She started to pull away, but something within her seemed to counter what her mind was screaming for her to do. Instead of pushing him away, she pulled back. Doing so caused her to lose her balance and fall back into an almost supine position.

He interpreted the action as an invitation and responded immediately. With his weight on his elbow, he leaned over her and kissed the hollow of her neck. His beard felt so much softer than she had expected. It tickled in the most exciting ways!

His tongue ran around the outside edge of her ear, sending tingles clear through her body. She felt his hand fumbling with a button on her blouse.

The realization of what he was doing shot sudden stabs of fear through her. What *was* he doing? Never mind! She knew perfectly well what he was doing, What was she doing? Why was she letting him do this?

The fear instantly became an almost blind terror. With strength born of that terror, she twisted out from under him and pushed him away.

'Wait!' she said. 'I ... I don't want to do this. Please.'

His eyes flashed with a fire that fueled her terror even more. She pulled further back away from him, struggling to refasten the button of her blouse that he had managed to undo, to regain a measure of control and composure.

She realized for the first time how truly far they were from the wagon train. Even if she screamed it was unlikely anyone would hear her from here. He was so strong! She had allowed him to become aroused, to believe she was willing to give herself to him. Now anger mingled with the desire in his eyes.

She cast about in her mind for some focus upon which to steady her swirling emotions. Something in her wanted to surrender herself to this wild mountain man. At the same time she was appalled that she could ever have such a desire.

She was a Christian woman! Even the level of her desire for Andrew caused guilt to blossom in her, though she knew it was natural. But its naturalness seemed easier, somehow, to control. Her feelings for this wild denizen of the wilderness was simply ... lust. Lust! That's exactly what it was. But instead of abhorrent, it felt almost irresistible.

God must surely understand her emotions, she thought wildly. He created them! If it were so wrong, why would she, a good Christian woman, have such feelings. If something felt so right somehow, how could it be as wrong as it surely must be? And if it were all that wrong, wouldn't God forgive her? Shouldn't she be allowed one 'slip'? Would it really be all that bad? Besides, neither Andrew nor anyone else would ever need to know. If nobody knew anyway, and God forgave her when she asked forgiveness, why would it be so terribly wrong?

Her scrambled thoughts twisted around each other in her mind, logic against emotion, deeply ingrained knowledge of right and wrong against intense desire, twisted reasoning making havoc of efforts to think clearly. She had to find a way to sort out all her tangled urges and restraints, and quickly.

'How ... how do the Indians survive all winter?' Hannah asked. The words sounded absurd, even to her. It didn't matter. She wasn't sure why, but she felt a sudden desperation to do something, anything, to turn the conversation, change the subject. His response was to gape uncomprehendingly.

'Huh?'

Speaking swiftly, as if to protect herself with a frantic torrent of words against him, she said,

'You said the Arapaho had a really long winter. How do they live through such a time without starving?'

He slid over close to where she had come to a sitting position. His hand slid around her waist.

'Oh, most of the time they stay in their tepees with a fire goin'. They got lots o' furs on the ground, to keep warm. An' they spend lots o' time like this, feelin' all these grand things you're feelin', wantin' each other just like you're wantin' me. You are the most beautiful woman I've ever seen in my whole life.'

As he talked he kept trying to undo the button she had tried so hard to get buttoned again, but had been frustrated in doing so because she was shaking. She pushed his hand away.

'But ... but they have to run out of food.' She determinedly pursued the subject.

He shrugged. 'They run short when the winter's long, all right. A lot o' the kids an' old folks don't make it, most winters.'

The casual way in which he said that jarred her to the core.

'What? Why would the children and the old people be the ones not to make it?'

'If there ain't food enough to go around, they're the ones that don't generally get enough to survive.'

'But ... but ... wouldn't the ... the adults go without, themselves, so their children could eat? Or the old people?'

He shook his head impatiently. 'It don't work that way. Just like in any other part o' nature, it's the strong an' the quick that survive. If some o' the kids don't make it, it ain't gonna destroy the tribe. They'll make plenty other babies, just so long as the strong ones survive. If some o' the old ones don't make it, that's just that much dead weight that won't be draggin' 'em down next winter. They already done 'most all the real livin' they're gonna do anyway. It's just the way it is.'

She gaped at him in appalled silence. His attitude, more than his words, repulsed her. They gave her the impetus to finally pull completely away from him and stand up. At last she got her blouse buttoned. The look in his eyes worried her, as if he were pondering grabbing her and forcing himself on her.

'You don't think that's right, do you?' she demanded. 'Isn't that just … well, savage?'

'Of course it is.' He shrugged. 'They have to live like savages or they won't survive. I didn't say it was right. I just said that's the way it is. Just like the women doin' most o' the work. If they didn't, the men wouldn't have the time or the energy to do enough huntin' and fishin' an' such to collect enough food to get 'em through the next winter. Not to mention fightin' agin' whoever attacks 'em. An' makin' enough babies to replace the ones that die.'

'It … it must be challenging, living all alone like you do, knowing that's the kind of people that are all around you.'

'O' course it is. But it's free, too. Wild and free. Free to do whatever I wanta do, without worryin' about what somebody else is gonna think about it. Just you watch and see. It won't be many days afore the freedom o' this wide-open country'll take hold of ya, an' you won't be holdin' back from doin' what you want to do so bad you can taste it. Then I'll show you what it feels like to be really wild and free, my pretty Rachel.'

'My name's Hannah.'

'Not to me. You are my beautiful Rachel, perfectly formed and irresistible.'

As he said it, he grabbed the back of her head and held her while he kissed her hard once again. Then he whirled and walked away. As he went he waved a hand and said, 'You better gather up them mushrooms an' get 'em back to your ma, afore we both decide we don't wanta wait a few more days.'

By the time she had regathered the mushrooms from the pile into which she had dumped them and folded the edges of her apron up around them, he was gone. She felt a surprising sense of emptiness and loss, mingled with a profound sense of relief. She wasn't sure which was the strongest.

She was suddenly unsure who or what she herself was. Would she soon invite him away alone with her, to share that wild freedom he had offered? The thought was less appalling than it ought to have been. In fact, she ached to open herself to it, experience it, live it. What would she think of herself afterward if she did? What would Andrew think if he knew she even had such thoughts?

Andrew's face appeared suddenly in her mind. The placid strength of his blue eyes contrasted sharply with the dark fire in those of the mountain man. One called to her with a pure love and a desire every bit as strong as everything that had been surging within her. The other called to a side of her she had never known existed, beckoning with a wild urgency that left her breathless.

CHAPTER 18

She needed to find Andrew! She couldn't explain why, even to herself, but she needed to find him, to touch him, to have his arms around her. She trembled uncontrollably inside, even though she appeared calm outwardly.

She spotted him talking with Frank. He held the reins of his horse. It was standing spraddle-legged, covered with sweat and lather, head hanging.

Frank turned and strode purposefully away. Andrew led his horse back toward his family's wagon. She ran to catch up.

'Andrew!'

He stopped and turned to her. His face was drawn and sweat-streaked.

'Hannah!'

He held out his arms to her. She rushed into them, oblivious to whomever might be watching. She hugged him fiercely.

'Hey! What's wrong, sweetheart?'

'Oh, Andrew! I'm so glad to see you. Andrew, I ... where have you been? What have you been doing?'

'We got problems,' he said.

'What? Why? What problems?'

'Them Arapaho ain't two or three days ahead of us. They're pertneart straight south of us. We're gonna be past 'em any time. Frank figures they aim to attack us from behind, where we ain't expecting 'em.'

'What? Indians are going to attack us? When? Why?'

'We just gotta get ready. Frank's gettin' things set up.'

Pounding hoofs of a running horse interrupted the conversation. Everybody's attention instantly fixed on the outrider from behind the wagon train as he caught up to the last wagon, then began passing them without slowing.

Frank stepped into the open, near the head of the slowly moving assemblage. The outrider spotted him at once. He slid his horse to a halt and leaped from the saddle. The outrider's voice was loud, so a good share of those close by heard him clearly.

'The army's comin', Frank.'

'What?'

'Cavalry's comin' up behind us. Must be about fifty of 'em. Ridin' at a fast trot, so they're hurryin' some. Quick time, or some such thing, I think they call it.'

Frank pursed his lips. He looked around at those who had rushed to hear what was going on.

'Well, keep everything movin'. No need to stop for the army. They can ride around us just fine, wherever they're goin'. Go ahead back to your post.'

Clearly disappointed that his news didn't inspire greater reaction, Dave mounted his horse and left at a trot.

Half an hour later the cavalry troop overtook them. They reined in to the side of the trail and continued, waving greetings to those who waved to them almost as if afraid their commander would see them doing so.

When the head of the column reached where Frank was, once again, standing in clear view, the lieutenant leading them spoke to the sergeant at his side. The sergeant instantly held up a hand and yelled,

'Company halt!'

The lieutenant dismounted, removed his glove and

extended his hand to Frank.

'Lieutenant Daniel P. Woodbury, at your service, sir.'

'Happy to meet you, Lieutenant. I'm Frank Cross, wagon master.'

'Have you had any incidents, Mr Cross?'

'Incidents?'

'Chiefly Indian attacks.'

'Nope. No problems at all. Should we have?'

'It is more likely that you are about to have,' the lieutenant said. 'Our Pawnee scouts have reported an Arapaho encampment in the vicinity that is … shall we say …"home" to a white renegade. The group has been responsible for attacks and wanton destruction on three wagon trains of which we are aware.'

'Three wagon trains?'

'Yes sir. They seem to pick smaller wagon trains, such as this one. They find a way to attack and overwhelm them almost without resistance. Then they drive both wagons and livestock to a location where they will not be found by those following the trail. At this point we are unaware of any survivors.'

A large group from the wagon train had already gathered around the two men. A gasp went up from all of them simultaneously.

'They kilt 'em all?' somebody questioned aloud.

'When they were eventually found by our scouts,' Woodbury responded, 'they were, of course, beyond showing whether they had been … uh … mutilated. The bones, of course, were well scattered by scavengers. Whatever remained of the wagons and their contents had been burned. We are not aware of any survivors.'

'What Indians?' a voice demanded.

'Arapaho. It seems to be a small to mid-sized village, led, or at least accompanied, as I said, by a white man.'

'What's he look like? This white man,' the same voice demanded.

'His name actually is Harvey Ridley. He fled and joined himself to this group of Arapaho to evade trial and imprisonment for a number of crimes. He goes mostly now by the name of Jeremiah Smith, or Jeremiah Moses, or Jedediah Hellcomb when in contact with white people. He has at least one Indian wife, and has, as we euphemistically say, "gone native".'

Another gasp went up from the assembled travelers. Ole Anderson spoke up.

'You just missed 'im, Lieutenant. He done lit out with his packhorse a-trailin' behind 'im right before our outrider let us know you was comin'.'

Woodbury's disappointment was visible.

'You still got a good chance at 'em, Lieutenant,' Frank said. 'One o' my best scouts found their camp. It ain't no more'n five miles due south o' where you are right now.'

The lieutenant whirled to face his sergeant.

'Sergeant, give the men thirty minutes for rest and coffee, or whatever this wagon train is prepared to offer by way of refreshments. Then we will head due south. When we commence, command all ahead double time. Send a man back to inform our supply and ammunition wagons. We may be able finally to catch up to this bunch.'

There were more instant offers of coffee and snacks than there were soldiers to accept them. They took full advantage of the time allowed them, then mounted up. As the column

swung in a smart left flank maneuver and headed south-
ward, Ole said,

'I seen that feller always a-watchin' everythin' everyone
did, watchin' who was herdin' the livestock, always a-studyin'
us. I knowed he wasn't all he said he was. I knowed it, I tell
ya.'

Standing with the group listening to the conversation,
Hannah leaned against Andrew. His arm went around her
waist. Both had a sense of just having survived a very real
threat to their lives. And to their budding relationship,
Hannah added silently.

CHAPTER 19

They were riding slowly, stirrup to stirrup. The herd of
animals belonging to the wagon train moved along meeting
little to hinder their progress, snatching up whatever grass
hadn't been eaten by previous wagon trains. This allowed
Hannah and Andrew to talk at length.

However, it was only after a lot of small talk, then a long
silence, that Hannah said, 'What's going to happen to them,
Andrew?'

'Who?'

'The Indians.'

It was less than a week since her narrow escape from
the mountain man, and the impostor's own narrow escape
from the troop of cavalry. They still had heard no word as to
whether that military unit had been successful in catching

up to the band of Arapaho Indians and the renegade mountain man, whose real name was, apparently, Harvey Ridley. Andrew had been careful not to mention the man or the incident to Hannah, waiting for her bring it up if and when she chose to do so.

He studied her closely out of the corner of his eye before he answered.

'Well, my guess is that the army hasn't even found them. Oh, I'm sure they found where they had been camped, but Smith, or Ridley, or whatever his name is, had a head start, and I'm bettin' he can move mighty fast when he has to. He'd have warned the Indian village. They can pack up and be gone in a couple hours, according to what I've heard. The army likely spent the next couple days figuring out in what direction they went, but they'll never catch up to them.'

'But I don't mean just them. I mean all the others.'

'What others? That's the only Indians we've had to deal with. So far, anyway.'

Hannah was again silent long enough for Andrew to wonder if she'd forgotten the question. She hadn't. She spoke slowly.

'Every two or three weeks we're in the territory of a different tribe of Indians, even if we don't see them or have to deal with them. But we're not their biggest problem. We're just passing through. We, and the other wagon trains, kill off the game and stuff close to the trail, but that's not a big problem, I wouldn't think. But when we all get to Oregon, aren't there going to be Indians there, too?'

'Well, sure. I guess.'

'And all these people, including us, will claim land to farm and ranch, until all the land is claimed by someone.

Everyone will build fences and make roads and build towns. Then what will the Indians do?'

'I don't know. Hadn't thought about it.'

'Maybe we should think about it, since we'll be part of the problem.'

Andrew really wanted to talk about other things, but he knew Hannah well enough by now to know that when she got something stuck in her craw, she wasn't going to be sidetracked. He cast around in his mind for a way to answer that would allay her concern, without sounding callous or shallow. It sounded almost lame to himself when he said, 'Maybe the Indians will just learn to farm and ranch, and become part of who lives there, like everybody else.'

'But will they? Or will they fight for their land and their way of life, and try to drive all of us white people back out?'

'Oh, they'll fight at first, most likely,' he conceded. 'But there's too many of us, and hundreds, maybe thousands more comin' behind us. The Indians can't win in the long run.'

'But then what happens to them?'

'Well, I guess the army'll finally force 'em to sign a treaty, like they did the Indians back East. Then the Indians will end up living on a reservation.'

'Then what do they do?'

The shrug of his shoulders indicated as much irritation at the direction of her questions as lack of any answer. His voice was almost gruff as he said, 'Live like they always have. Just in that one area.'

'But they can't live in just a small area, the way they live now,' she protested. 'It'll only take a little while until all the game in that area is gone, then what?'

'Well, back East the government's appointed an Indian agent to look after each reservation. He makes sure everyone has food and stuff. Whatever they need. One treaty I heard about, the government promised to provide for the tribe's descendants for seven generations.'

'Which probably means the Indian agent will steal half of what's supposed to go to the Indians. But suppose he's an honest, conscientious person and does his job right. So then the Indians do nothing, and the government provides everything they need?'

'Sure.'

'How terrible!'

'Whatd'ya mean, "how terrible"? What's terrible about that? I'd love to have a deal like that!'

'Would you really? Andrew, what would you do if you had nothing that you really needed to do, all day, every day? What would you do if you didn't have to work, or take care of livestock, or farm a piece of ground, or do anything but eat and sleep?'

'Get fat and lazy, that's what.'

'And what of your children? If they grew up without ever having to do anything to earn a living, what would they be able to do?'

It was Andrew's turn to become silent, thoughtful. After a long while he said, 'I hadn't even thought that far. I guess if that went on for two or three generations, nobody would even know how to do anything at all.'

'Or want to do anything at all,' she added. 'Except be taken care of. And they'd feel justified in being taken care of, because they'd had their way of life taken away from them.'

99

'That's true,' he conceded. 'And then there's always the whiskey.'

Her eyebrows rose. 'What about the whiskey?'

'One of the reasons they have so much trouble with trading posts and such, is that Indians really, really like whiskey. It seems to have some special hold on them, for some reason. If they can get a-hold of any, they drink themselves senseless, and stay drunk as long as the whiskey lasts. Once they get their first taste of it, they'll do almost anything to get more. So there's always someone willing to sneak whiskey to 'em, and make money doing it.'

'I don't understand that. Where would the Indians get any money?'

'They don't need money. The whiskey smugglers will trade them out of their horses, or trade them a dollar's worth of whiskey for five dollars' worth of flour or corn meal or blankets or whatever the government's provided 'em, till they don't have anything left to trade.'

'So if they never have to sober up, never have to do anything, they'll just become worse and worse ... drunkards.'

'And when they don't have anything left to trade for more whiskey, they'll go on the warpath or something to get it, or to get something to trade for it.'

'So making them live on reservations and taking care of them will end up being the worst thing in the world that could possibly be done to them.'

He stared off into the distance, absently watching the livestock they'd herded for a long time. He took a deep breath and let it out slowly.

'It would seem so.'

'That is so ... so ... not fair!'

Again his shrug communicated more irritation than confusion.

'Life is never fair. But it's always been like that, the world over.'

'What do you mean?'

'Remember your history lessons? Any time someone defeats another people, the ones that lose have to go somewhere else, if they have someplace else to go. Then they have to fit in there.'

'I remember wondering about that,' Hannah replied. 'It seemed strange to me that when the Israelites were carried off into captivity, the prophets told them to live peaceably there, become part of those people, and pray for the place where they were forced to live.'

'That was their only reasonable solution,' Andrew agreed. 'Try to fit in and become part of the people that defeated them. Either that or just keep fighting until they were all dead.'

'But because we're a Christian people, we won't just force the Indians to do that. Fit in and live like white people, I mean.'

'Nope. We really can't do that. Most people wouldn't stand for it. We're Christians, so we love not just our neighbors. Jesus told us to love our enemies too. So we try to do what he said. And the way we do that is to put the Indians on reservations and take care of them. And in the end that's worse than telling them to adapt or die. Some of 'em would die if we did that, but most of 'em would learn to adapt.'

'But their whole way of life will be gone.'

'True. But that might not be all bad. Think about that. Instead of living in a hide tent, freezing every winter, going through what they call "the starving time" before spring gets here, they'd learn to live in real houses, store up food for winter, be warm and not have to watch their old folks and children die in every year's starving time. They wouldn't be carrying their water in animal bladders or chewing hides to make them soft enough to make clothes, or drinking out of the same mud holes their animals are standing in.'

'It's still stealing their way of life away from them.'

'But it can't be helped. It's the manifest destiny of our people to civilize this land.'

'Our ancestors should've just stayed in Europe or England or Ireland or wherever.'

'They couldn't. They still can't. There's already more people there than the land can support, so folks are starving to death there. And here's this huge country over on this side of the ocean that will support a thousand times more people than there are in it now. There's no way those crowded, starving people aren't going to come swarming to this country.'

'So there's no real answer. There's just too many people in the world.'

'We're gettin' way too deep in the philosophy end of this whole subject. How'd we get into this discussion anyway?'

'I just started wondering what was going to happen to those Indians. There has to be something better than forcing them onto reservations.'

'Nobody's figured out what, if there is.'

'Well they better get it figured out.'

Neither of them had any confidence that that was going to happen any time soon. They rode almost without conversation until they were relieved by the next herders. Hannah lay awake thinking about it far into the night.

CHAPTER 20

'Another mountain man?'

Andrew's face clearly displayed a whole range of emotions that his words barely hinted at.

'This guy is someone Frank knows.'

'How does, Frank know him?' Hannah was clearly confused. Andrew shrugged only slightly.

'He says he's run into him on two or three trips he's already made with wagon trains.'

'What does he want?'

'He says he wants to join up with us all the way to Oregon.'

'Why?' Her voice was harsher than she intended.

Andrew and Hannah were, as was their custom, riding together to herd the loose cattle and horses along with the wagon train. The animals were all well accustomed to the routine, so it was mostly a matter of following along behind them and keeping them grouped. That allowed them plenty of time to ride stirrup to stirrup and talk.

Andrew's eyebrows arched at the harshness in Hannah's voice. He felt as if he were defending somebody he didn't know when it wasn't his job to defend him.

'Same reason the other guy gave, but for some reason Frank believes this one. The fur trade's kinda goin' to pot. The Indian tribes are movin' around more, on account o' the pressure from so many white people movin' through. A lot o' people are stayin' in the country, tryin' to settle a place close to one o' the forts.'

'Like the Quincy family that left our train at Ash Hollow?'

'Yeah. Just like them. There's already half a dozen

families that've decided to settle along Whitetail Crick, and the Quincys decided to join 'em.'

'I think that's just foolish. We already know how good things are in Oregon, and it's settled enough for us not to be in constant danger from Indians.'

'Yeah, but Frank couldn't convince the Quincys of that.'

'So while they decided to stay there, this guy wants to do just the opposite.'

'So it seems.'

'What's his name?'

'Buck Wilson. Or so he says.'

Hannah picked up the skepticism in Andrew's voice instantly.

'You don't believe him?'

Andrew shrugged. 'I don't have any reason not to believe 'im, I guess.'

'But you don't anyway.' It was a statement, not a question.

'Anyone can throw out a name and claim that's him.'

'So why would he use a made-up name?'

'Could be any number o' reasons.'

'Like what?'

'Just like that Smith guy. Maybe he don't want people knowin' who he used to be or what he's done.'

'I think you're just too suspicious because we got fooled once.'

'Well, gettin' fooled once almost got us all killed.'

Hannah shuddered in spite of trying to hide her feelings.

'I know,' she said softly.

Andrew took a deep breath. His tone of voice changed. He clearly wanted to talk of other things. That was certainly all right with Hannah. In a voice just a trace too loud,

Andrew said, 'Anyway, Frank endorses this guy, so I guess that's all we need to know.'

'Speaking of the devil ...' Hannah said.

Andrew's head jerked up. His eyes darted to where Hannah was looking. From behind them the subject of their conversation trotted easily on his motley colored horse, obviously heading toward them.

'Mornin', folks,' he said as he approached. 'Nice day.'

'Couldn't ask for nicer,' Andrew agreed. Hannah remained silent.

'I'm Buck Wilson. I guess I'm gonna be joinin' you folks on to Oregon.'

'So we heard,' Andrew responded. 'Buck's kinda a different name, ain't it?'

The mountain man grinned. 'Oh, that ain't my real name. I don't never try to use my real name.'

'Why not?' Hannah demanded, without realizing how brash the question sounded.

Buck laughed. 'You ain't bashful about askin' questions, are you?'

Hannah blushed, but refused to back down. 'A name can't be all that bad.'

'You don't think so?'

'No.'

'Well, that's because you don't know what my real name is.'

'So what is it?'

Wilson regarded her with open amusement. 'I don't rightly remember anyone bein' that nosy and that determined all at the same time.'

'You're dodging the question,' Hannah insisted.

'Hannah! You're being rude,' Andrew remonstrated.

Hannah's chin thrust forward. 'Well, we were almost all killed because a mountain man that joined up with us didn't give us his real name. I don't think we ought to make the same mistake twice.'

The twinkle didn't leave Wilson's eyes. 'And what makes you think if I told you my real name that I'd be telling the truth?'

'I … I don't know. I guess I couldn't tell.'

'Oh, I 'spect you likely could, if I told you my real name. Nobody'd make it up.'

'So what is it?'

Buck laughed aloud. 'You just don't give up, do you?'

'No.'

'OK, then. It's Syzygus.'

Both Andrew and Hannah stared open-mouthed.

'It's what?' Hannah demanded.

Openly amused, Wilson said, 'See. I told you nobody'd make it up. My real name is Syzygus Wilson.'

'Where did your parents find a name like that?'

'Hannah!' Andrew scolded again. 'I think you should just drop it and remember your manners.'

Wilson held up a hand. 'Don't worry about it. It ain't that I'm ashamed of it or nothin'. It just causes a whole long explanation every time someone finds out what it is. My folks found it in the Bible, and it struck my pa's fancy, so they tagged it onto me. They told me it means "yokefellow" or "yokemate" or somethin' like that, and he was a friend of St Paul's in the Bible.

'Only mentioned once, I guess, and the smart guys argue about whether it's really a guy's name or just someone Paul called his "yokefellow" or "fellow worker" in his work. Now ... satisfied?'

Hannah opened and closed her mouth several times. Suddenly chagrined, she cast her eyes down.

'I ... I'm sorry. I was being really rude. But thank you for telling us, anyway. And I promise I won't tell a soul.' She giggled unexpectedly. 'Syzygus is really a strange name. But I really won't tell.'

'Yes you will,' Buck argued, a large grin festooned on his face. 'You'll just swear them all to silence before you tell 'em. Then it won't count, 'cause it'll just give you the help of all them other folks to keep your secret.'

Hannah flushed brilliantly. 'You're making fun of me.'

'Yup. That's what you get for being so nosy.'

Unsure how to answer, and suddenly very uncomfortable, Hannah said, 'I think I better catch up with the wagons.'

She reined her horse around and galloped away, ignoring Andrew's efforts to call her back.

Halfway to the wagons she decided it was an excellent opportunity to duck into a heavy stand of timber to relieve herself. She cast a quick look around to be sure nobody was about, then dismounted and walked a short distance into the copse. She returned quickly to her horse and prepared to mount.

'Well, now! Hello beautiful Rachel!'

She gasped and whirled at the unexpected voice behind her. Jeremiah Smith stood before her, a wicked smile on his face.

'How ... how did you get here?' she stammered.

'A-horseback. Same as you.' He smirked.

'But ... but you ... but the army was ... How did you get

away from the army?'

He laughed. 'Them guys couldn't find their own rear ends with both hands. We was packed up an' long gone afore they ever got where we'd been camped. We gave 'em enough of a false trail for their scouts to head 'em off in the wrong direction lookin' for us.'

She stared, speechless, for a long moment. Fear suddenly surged up within her, eclipsing her curiosity and surprise.

'What ... what are you doing here?'

'Aw, I just couldn't quit the country without the most beautiful woman I've run across in many a year. I just had to come back for my beautiful Rachel. I ain't aimin' to wait no seven years like Jacob did, though. You and me, we're gonna just up an' run off together today.'

'What!? We're ... I'm doing no such thing! How dare you!'

'Shut up your pretty face an' get on your horse. You're comin' with me. I done decided you're gonna be my white wife an' help my Arapaho wife with the work. An' with keepin' me happy, by the way.'

'Why ... you ... you... I'm not going anywhere with you. Now leave me alone.'

She didn't even see the blow coming. The back of Smith's hand connected with her jaw with stunning force. She sat down abruptly. The trees and brush spun wildly around her. Her head roared. She couldn't think.

Rough hands grabbed her and pulled her to her feet. She was dimly aware of being forced to mount her horse. She swayed in the saddle, fighting for balance. Her hands were swiftly bound to the saddle horn. Her feet were tied to the stirrups, which were tied to each other with a rope stretched beneath the horse's belly, so she could ride but she couldn't dismount. She was less than comfortable.

Her captor mounted his own horse and moved beside her, standing so that they were face to face. He stared at her until her eyes were able to focus on him.

'Now you got your choice, beautiful Rachel.' He smiled at her, as if they were having a friendly conversation. 'You can promise to keep your mouth shut, or I'll stuff a rag in it and tie it in place. That gets plumb awful uncomfortable, an' we got a long ride ahead, so I'd hate to do that if I don't have to.'

He waited for several breaths to let his words soak in through her confusion and the after-effects of the blow he had delivered to her face. When he was satisfied she understood, he spoke again.

'So are you gonna promise to keep quiet?' he demanded.

Her mind raced. What choice did she have? If she refused she'd have to ride with a rag stuffed in her mouth. Probably a dirty rag, all things considered. Even if she screamed, who would hear her? Finally she nodded, moving her head carefully to keep the dizziness from returning.

'Noddin' your pretty head ain't enough,' he snarled. 'I want you to say it.'

'I ... I'll be quiet,' she promised.

He rewarded the promise with one quick nod of his head.

'Fair enough. But if you make a peep I'll beat the livin' snot outa you afore I gag you. Don't forget it.'

He tied the ends of her horse's reins in a knot, lifted them over the horse's head, and hooked them over her saddle horn. Then he tied a length of rope to one of her horse's bit rings and secured the other end of it with a bowline knot around his own horse's neck.

Without another word he turned his own horse and kicked him into action. It had walked only a few yards before Hannah's horse understood that it was being led. It matched the pace of the mountain man's horse and followed willingly behind, oblivious to the disaster that had overtaken its rider.

After stopping at the edge of the trees and looking all directions for a long moment, the mountain man kicked his horse into action again. They forded the Platte River and headed directly north, keeping to low ground, largely out of sight of any eyes that might chance to be looking.

Hannah's heart sunk. They were going in the wrong direction! Even if anyone figured out where she had disappeared from, they'd send a search party on the south side of the river, and go the wrong way. But that would never happen. Nobody would have any idea what had happened to her. She could think of no way out of being doomed to being owned, forced to become part of an Indian tribe.

She promised herself she would never stop watching and waiting for an opportunity to escape, even if it took years.

CHAPTER 21

'What do you mean, she's not here?' Andrew demanded. 'She headed this way two hours ago.'

Frances Henford stared hard at him. 'I thought she was herding the livestock with you.'

'She was, but she got kinda upset when … Wilson was

razzin' her some. She said she was headin' back to the wagons.'

'Well, she never got here.'

'She had to've got here. Where else would she go?'

'I don't know, but she hasn't been here.'

'Something must have happened to her.'

'What would have happened?'

'I don't know. Maybe she fell off her horse, or it ran away with her, or … or … I don't know.'

Andrew and Hannah's mother looked helplessly at each other, neither offering any possible solution. Finally her mother said,

'Go find Frank. He'll know what to do.'

'Where is he?'

'I think he's just a couple wagons ahead talking with the Callahans. He was a while ago anyway.'

Andrew leaped into the saddle and spurred his horse on a dead run, passing the intervening wagons, causing raised eyebrows and alarming the occupants of those wagons.

'Hey, hey! What's the hurry?' Frank demanded, stepping out from between two wagons. Andrew skidded his horse to a halt.

'Hannah's missing!' he yelled, as if Frank were 200 yards away, instead of three feet in front of him.

'Whatd'ya mean, missing?'

'I mean she's missing. She left where we was herdin' the livestock and said she was comin' back to her wagon, but she didn't never get here.'

'You don't say. How long ago?'

'Couple hours.'

'Hmm. Too long to just be dallyin'. She wouldn'ta gone

off huntin', tryin' to stalk a deer or somethin' like some fella might've. Nobody's seen 'er?'

'I don't know. Her mother hasn't, anyway.'

'Well, don't get too excited. I'll send word up and down the wagons, see if anyone's seen 'er.'

'I'll ask all the wagons behind us,' Andrew replied, even as he whirled his horse and started back along the lumbering line of slow-moving conveyances. As he passed each one he yelled,

'Have you seen Hannah in the last couple hours?'

At every wagon he received the same response. 'No, we ain't seen 'er. Did somethin' happen to 'er?'

Ignoring the reply Andrew kept moving, asking the same question over and over. With every negative answer he grew more worried.

At the end of the line of wagons he whirled his horse and galloped back to the Henford Conestoga.

'Did you find her?' Frances called as he approached.

'No!'

Before he could say any more Will Henford approached, walking swiftly.

'What's this about Hannah bein' missin'?' he demanded.

Andrew lifted both hands in a helpless gesture.

'I don't know where she went,' he said. 'She was with me for the early mornin', herding of the livestock. About the time we were replaced by the next guys, this mountain man stopped by to talk. We got to razzin' Hannah, an' she rode off. She said she was coming back to your wagon. But she never got here.'

'You ask around, to see if anyone's seen 'er?'

'I asked all the wagons behind you. Frank's checking

with all the wagons ahead of you.'

'You ain't seen 'er at all, Fannie?' Will asked. Frances shook her head.

'I thought she was still with Andrew.'

'Here comes Frank,' Andrew announced. 'It looks like Wilson's with him.'

The pair rode up at a swift trot.

'Any sign of 'er?' Frank demanded, even before they were abreast of the Henford wagon.

'No,' Andrew said. 'No sign of her up front?'

'None. We'd best figure out where she went. Was she mad enough when she left you boys to ride off somewhere in a huff?'

'No,' Andrew said again. 'She was a little peeved, but kinda laughin' underneath at the same time she was actin' peeved. It was almost time for our spell o' watchin' the live-stock to be over, so I thought she was just comin' back to the wagon. That's what she said she was doin'.'

'Time's wastin',' the mountain man interjected. 'We'd best be findin' out what happened to 'er.'

Beneath Andrew's response was a sense of total futility and emptiness.

'How?'

'Track 'er,' Wilson responded.

'You can do that?' Andrew marveled.

'O' course. Unless her tracks is muddled up somehow. Let's head back to where she left us, an' follow 'er.'

'You and Andrew do that,' Frank ordered. 'Once you figure it out, come tell me afore you go lookin' for 'er.'

'Let's go,' Buck said, kicking his horse to a swift trot.

Andrew stared at Frank for a long moment, as if frozen in

indecision. Frank's voice was gruff as he spoke.

'So git goin'. Stick with Buck, an' let him call the shots. I know you got no way to know jack squat about trackin', but Buck can track a mouse across a flat rock an' clear into a snake's belly if he has to. Now git goin'!'

Andrew turned his horse and kicked him into a gallop to catch up with the rapidly receding figure in buckskins. By the time he caught up with him they were halfway to where Hannah had left them.

'Can you really track her through grass an' stuff. Like them guys in dime novels an' such?'

'Ain't never read no dime novels,' Buck responded. 'But yeah. I can track.'

Neither spoke until they had returned to where the three of them had talked together. Buck rode in a wide circle, then said, 'This way.'

Still riding at a swift trot he followed a path that led directly toward where the wagons would have been at that point. Then he abruptly turned aside from the direction they had been following and headed toward a thick patch of willows, cottonwoods and chokeberry bushes.

'Now where's she goin?' Andrew demanded.

'Hard to say. I'm guessin' she headed for that brush to relieve herself, outa sight o' everyone.'

'Oh.'

As they approached the two-acre patch of cover, the mountain man said,

'Uh-oh. That ain't good.'

'What ain't good?'

'Stay put, so there ain't no more tracks gettin' in the way,' Wilson commanded.

He dismounted, walked into the copse and squatted down, studying the ground. He moved from time to time, looking at something only he could decipher. The best Andrew could see was that some brush and grass was somewhat trampled.

Wilson returned to his horse and mounted. Without a word he rode through the trees and brush and headed straight north. When they came to the Platte River he waded his horse across and continued northward for several hundred yards. Only then did he stop and turn to Andrew.

'Let's get back to the wagons.'

'What's goin' on?' Andrew demanded. Wilson simply shook his head.

'I'll tell you an' Frank at the same time.'

He kicked his horse into a long lope, heading back to the river. They crossed it and Wilson headed for the wagons. Andrew's horse seemed to know he needed to keep up. That was fortunate. Andrew was too confused and worried to think even that clearly.

Frank saw them coming and loped out to meet them. Buck reined in and waited until Andrew caught up. Then he began his explanation.

'It looks like she headed back to the wagons, all right. Then she stopped in a bunch o' trees. Prob'ly needed to relieve 'erself. Someone surprised 'er there. Knocked 'er down. Maybe knocked 'er out. Then he stuck 'er on her horse. Stomped around some doin' it, so I'm guessin' he tied her on. Then they took off, him a-leadin' her horse. They crossed the river an' headed straight north.'

Frank's brow furrowed increasingly as the mountain man offered his explanation. When the mountain man fell silent he said, 'Who?'

Wilson shrugged.

'Indian, maybe, but not likely. Wears moccasins though. Horse ain't shod. Moves a lot like an Indian, but not quite. One Indian wouldn'ta been alone, like that. It looks like someone was watchin', just waitin' for a chance to grab the girl. I didn't take time to backtrack him afore he was in that clump o' trees, so I can't say that for sure.'

'Smith!' Andrew spit out the word as if it were a curse. Frank's eyebrows rose.

'The guy that was here?'

Andrew's mind was racing.

'He wore moccasins. His horse ain't shod. An' he had a thing for Hannah. He tried to… to take advantage of her when he tricked her into going with him to gather mush-rooms that time. He was really turnin' on the charm till then. She pertneart had to fight her way away from him then.'

'I'd 've thought him and his bunch of Arapaho buddies would be runnin' like coyotes to get away from the army,' Frank mused.

'Not likely,' Buck disagreed. 'From what you told me, he had plenty o' time to let 'em know the army was comin'. They'd have left a false trail in one direction and gone off in another. It'd be just his style to slip back around an' grab the girl, just to let us know he could. And if he was all infatuated with 'er, that'd be all it'd take for him to do it.'

'You know this guy, then?'

'I know him.'

'Where would he take her, if it was him?'

Buck thought about it a long moment.

'He headed north. My guess'd be somewhere in the Wildcat Hills. Since the army thinks that band of Arapahos went south, they likely went north instead. There's a whole area of pine timber and canyon country, straight north o' Chimney Rock an' Scottsbluff, maybe forty, fifty miles. They could hide out in that country for months without the army bein' able to find 'em, unless they had Indian scouts.'

'They didn't have any Indian scouts with them when they were here,' Frank confirmed.

'So what are we going to do?' Andrew demanded. 'We can't just let 'im have her!'

Frank looked at Buck, eyebrows raised. Buck pursed his lips thoughtfully.

'I don't think he'll be all that hard to follow. I know the man. He thinks he's a better Indian than the Indians, but he ain't really half as good as he thinks he is.'

'I can send half a dozen men with you,' Frank offered instantly. Buck shook his head.

'Too many. One or two people might be able to follow him and slip up on him in a way that wouldn't give him time to kill the girl. More than that's too hard to stay hid an' move fast at the same time.'

'I'm going with you,' Andrew insisted immediately.

Buck gave him a long, openly appraising look. Instead of addressing Andrew, however, he spoke to the wagon master.

'Is he capable o' bein' more help than hindrance?' he asked.

Andrew flushed angrily, but held his tongue. Frank imitated Buck's look of appraisal. After what seemed to Andrew like far too much time, he said, 'A couple months ago I'd have said: not a chance. The boy learns real fast, though.

He's one of my advance scouts now, an' does a real fine job of it. He was already around behind that Jeremiah Smith guy afore he got to where he could talk to me. That says somethin' for 'im. If he'll listen to you an' do what you tell 'im, he'd be a good man to have along.'

'Fair enough,' Buck agreed. He turned to address Andrew directly. 'Get your bedroll, a handgun an' a rifle, three times as much ammunition as you think you could possibly need, an' enough grub to live off for a week or three. We ain't gonna be shootin' no game, to let our gunshots announce our position, so what you got with you is all you're gonna have to eat. Be ready to leave in twenty minutes.'

Twice Andrew opened his mouth to speak, but closed it both times. Frank and Buck had turned away from him and were discussing plans for what they were going to do, where and how either one could leave messages on the trail to expedite a reunion, and what their chances were of success.

Instead of entering the conversation Andrew whirled his horse and galloped to his own family's wagon. He got ready to go with five minutes to spare.

CHAPTER 22

Her hands ached. She moved them as much as the ropes binding her to the saddle horn would allow. It wasn't enough to relieve the cramps caused by muscles being held in one position with restricted blood flow. They hurt so badly she wanted to scream.

Her legs and feet hurt almost as much. She could shift her weight in the saddle and twist her feet into different positions, within the restriction of the binding ropes, but it wasn't enough to relieve her misery. The pain radiated upward from her feet and ankles, through her legs, into her lower back. She had never in her life hurt so much in so many places at once.

Jeremiah Smith, or whatever his name was, hadn't spoken since they crossed the Platte River. They rode for a time through rolling sand hills, keeping to low ground as much as possible. Because all the valleys in those sand hills ran mostly east and west, it was necessary for them to cross hills and ridges regularly. Each time they did so Smith chose a spot that was the lowest visible point to cross over into the next valley.

Under different circumstances she would have been entranced by the country they rode through. It was absolutely beautiful. Except for an almost total absence of trees of any kind, it was lush with life. Tall grass rippled and flowed in the breeze, giving the endless undulating hills an impression of some great grass ocean, stretching in all directions.

In every valley they crossed stood ponds of water. Some were shallow and small. Others were sizeable lakes, necessitating a detour of a couple of miles.

Every body of water of any size supported waterfowl of every description. Ducks with more variety in their plumage than anything she could have imagined shared the water with several varieties of geese. None of the geese were quite as large as the cranes that had so awed her on the Platte River, but they were large, none the less.

Groups of deer watched their approach warily, but stood their ground.

Antelopes were less brave, but almost always she could see one or more groups of the fleet animals eyeing them from some spot of high ground.

Buffalo wallowed in the shallows of several of the small lakes, churning the ground into vast mud pits where the great beasts sought refuge from the clouds of deer flies and heel flies.

Those were the insects that bedeviled her the most. Through the low-lying areas the mosquitoes hovered in swarms that threatened to bleed her dry. She could not swat them or swish them away. She could only endure their bites until she felt as if every part of her body was covered with the itching punctures they left behind.

Eventually they even bothered Smith so much that he paused to do something about them. He veered away from the path they seemed to be following to a large patch of sagebrush. He stripped off a large amount of the leaves and stuffed them into a buckskin bag that hung from a strap slung over his shoulder.

He mounted up again and rode to the edge of a lake. Taking great handfuls of the soupy mud from the water's edge, he mixed and ground the sage leaves into it, then smeared it on face and hands until all his exposed skin was covered.

He had started to mount his horse again when he looked at Hannah. Her swollen face and arms signalled her misery more eloquently than words could have done. The mountain man shrugged his shoulders, repeated the concoction of the salve and strode across to her. He smeared it on her face, her arms and hands, and the back of her neck. He took advantage of the opportunity to grope her enough to make her whimper and cringe in protest, but less than she had feared he might.

She needed to empty her bladder so badly its discomfort almost eclipsed all her other aches and pains, but she had no idea if she dared ask for an opportunity to do anything about it.

The effect of the fragrant mudpack was heavenly! It cooled the fierce itching of a thousand tiny bites. It lessened her misery enough to revive her awareness of the pain in her hands, her feet, her back. Even they were preferable to the overwhelming torture of the mosquito and deer-fly bites. She considered thanking her captor, but opted instead for the silence to which she had foresworn herself.

Abruptly, in the middle of one broad valley, Smith stopped and dismounted. He stood beside his horse and relieved himself with no attempt at modesty. He started to remount, then once again looked questioningly at his captive. He strode back to where she sat her horse.

'You gotta be just about as ready to bust as I was,' he said. 'I'll take you loose an' let you drain out if you promise not to try nothin'.'

In spite of her determination to say nothing, her desperation forced her to speak.

'I ... I won't run or anything.'

He eyed her carefully for a long moment, then nodded his head. Without another word he removed the tethers from her feet, then untied her hands. Her hands especially were instantly stabbed with intense pain. Trying her best to ignore it, she flexed her fingers and wrists, forcing the circulation back into them, until the pain began to subside.

She slid from the saddle, then gripped it tightly to keep from falling. Her legs and feet hurt just as badly as her hands, refusing to bear her weight. As soon as she thought she could, she stepped away from her horse, staggering, but maintaining enough balance to remain standing. She looked inquiringly at her captor. He waved a hand.

'Well, git with it, if'n you're gonna. We ain't stoppin' no longer'n necessary.'

She stared at him, refusing to believe he intended to watch her. Finally she said,

'Would you … turn around?'

He laughed, one short, harsh sound that held no mirth.

'Not a chance, beautiful Rachel. I'm gonna be watchin' you day'n' night from now on. Get used to it.'

Her mind raced in a turmoil of emotions and needs of equal intensity. She had to relieve the pressure in her bladder, which had grown intolerable. She could not expose herself to this … this crude animal. But she had no choice. If she didn't take advantage of this opportunity, she knew another would not come for a long while. Yet she simply could not.

In the end she turned her back to him and did what nature required her to do. When she finished she stepped back to her horse. She looked at him, cringing at the crude grin with which he favored her.

'If … if you don't tie me, I … I won't try to do anything.'

He stared at her for a long moment, until she said,

'Please?'

The plaintive note in her voice made her feel ashamed, but she couldn't help it. She stared imploringly at him.

After what seemed like an eternity he shrugged his shoulders. He gathered up the two pieces of rawhide rope he had used to tie her and stuffed them into that buckskin bag slung over his shoulder.

'If you do try somethin', you'll be sorrier'n you ever been about anything you ever did. You understand?' he demanded.

'I won't,' was the only thing she could think of to say. Her voice sounded as meek and helpless as she felt.

It was worth it, though. Even with him still leading her horse, it was heavenly to be able to move about freely in the saddle.

Nevertheless, she was so exhausted she was swaying in the saddle before he gave any indication of stopping. A great white circle of a moon rose in the east more than an hour before the sun disappeared in the west. The light of that moon was more than sufficient to show them their way. They rode on into the night for another two hours before the renegade mountain man finally reined in and slid off his horse.

They were in a saddle in a long ridge of the endless sand hills, high enough to be away from the water holes that marked nearly all the valleys and swales, and the insects were noticeably less numerous. He stripped the saddle off her horse, hobbling the animal's front feet together with one of the ropes he had used to tie her to the saddle. Then he removed the bridle as well.

He did the same with his own horse, hobbling it too. He threw her saddle blanket to her.

'We'll sleep a little while,' he said.

She gripped the saddle blanket as she felt the blood drain from her face. What was he going to do now? Would he force himself on her now, before they rode any further? Would he wait until she was asleep, then throw himself on her? Would he wait until they met up with the band of Indians he had become part of, then rape her in plain view of the rest of them, as she had heard was often the fate of white captive women?

He simply dropped onto the ground, curled up, and covered himself with the blanket that served as his saddle. With no choice but to follow suit, she walked just a little way away and did the same.

She thought she would remain awake all night in fear of what he might do. She underestimated the depth of her own exhaustion. She was asleep in minutes.

CHAPTER 23

'I don't know how you can tell where we're going.'

Riding at a swift trot, conversation was difficult, but Andrew could not contain himself any longer. Buck Wilson had led out at this pace, supposedly following the trail of the renegade mountain man who called himself Jeremiah Smith, and his captive. Andrew had forced himself to ride in silence, trusting the expertise of the man who was essentially a stranger to him. He felt he had to do so because the wagon master had said he should. He also knew he himself had no ability whatever to find Hannah, or even to know where to look. Now, however, the churning in his stomach forced him to speak.

Without turning his head or slackening his pace, the mountain man said,

'See where that grass is bent down?'

'A lot of grass is bent down.'

'Yeah, but not in a line. The rest of it is just random little patches where something lay down on it, or the wind hit it wrong. But some of it is bent in spot after spot that makes a line.'

'I can't see it.'

'Not surprising. Stop lookin' so close to you, an' look up ahead. Look for somethin' that looks like a little different shape in the grass, that goes on for a ways.'

'I saw that a while back, for a little ways. Then I couldn't see it any more.'

'Keep tryin'. The more you work at it, the better you get.'

'How far ahead of us are they?'

'Four hours. Maybe five. But he don't seem to be in a big hurry.'

'Why not?'

'He likely figures there ain't nobody in the wagon train that can track, so he don't have to worry none about anyone comin' after 'im.'

Andrew pondered this thought for a long while. Silently he acknowledged that had this mountain man, Wilson, not appeared, desirous of joining the wagon train, Smith would have been right. The only one in the whole train with any experience in this part of the country was Frank, and he was the wagon master. He couldn't leave the wagon train under any circumstances, even though he was capable of tracking.

'We need to let the horses drink,' Buck announced.

Andrew frowned.

'Hadn't we oughta just keep hurryin', so we can catch up to 'em?'

He would have laughed had he seen his own appearance in a mirror. After being bedeviled by the mosquitoes and deer flies in the first couple of valleys of the sand hills, Wilson had resorted to the same tactic as Smith had employed for himself and Hannah. Smeared with the aromatic mud, nothing showed on their faces but the round circles of their eyes, though Wilson knew enough not to coat themselves too thickly with the substance. It was necessary only to leave enough of it on their skin for the insects to smell and avoid. Even so, they looked like children who had been playing in the mud. Buck shook his head.

'It's gonna be a long ride. Then there's no tellin' what we're gonna ride into. We may need to outrun some band of Indians, or 'most anything. We gotta keep our horses as fresh as we can.'

'But he ain't stoppin', is he?'

'He ain't yet, anyhow.'

'So maybe he'll wear out their horses sooner, an' we can catch 'em?'

'Maybe.'

A hundred other questions rattled around in Andrew's mind, but he hesitated to ask any of them. Mostly he was afraid they would further betray his own ignorance and incompetence.

They stopped at the edge of one of the many small lakes that seemed almost omnipresent in the valleys. As the horses drank, Buck dug into one of his saddlebags and brought out a couple handfuls of grain, putting them into his hat. He then offered the hat to his horse, who greedily scarfed the grain down.

Trying hard to act as if it were something he himself might have thought of, Andrew followed suit. After his horse had scoured every last kernel of oats from his hat, he quailed at the thought of putting the hat back on his head.

Buck had already remounted. His expression signaled impatience at Andrew's slowness. Noting this, Andrew clapped the hat onto his head and stepped into the saddle. He had to lope for a ways to catch up with Buck.

'They'll have to stop when it gets dark, won't they?' he asked at one point. Buck shook his head.

'It ain't gonna get dark for a while. The moon's already up. Full moon. Gonna be plenty light to keep ridin' till about the time the moon sets.'

Sudden despair gave Andrew's voice a tentative tone.

'Can you track'em by moonlight?'

'As long as it don't cloud up. Matter o' fact, the angle o' the moonlight can make the trail up ahead easier to see.'

As they neared the ridge between each valley Buck always slid off his saddle, removed his hat, and crawled to the top of the hill. Only after surveying what lay on the other side did he proceed.

'Still headin' almost straight north,' he observed on one occason as he remounted his horse. 'Startin' to swing a little west, though.'

'Why would he do that?'

'Depends on where he's headin'. If he's headin' for the Wildcat Hills, he needs to get farther west. I don't know why he's waited so long to do it, unless there's somethin' to the west he's bein' careful to avoid until he's north of it.'

'What could that be?'

Wilson shrugged. 'Who knows? Different bunch of Indians, maybe. The army bunch that's after 'em, maybe. Hydrophoby skunk country, maybe.'

'Hydrophoby skunk country? What's that?' Andrew took the bait instantly.

'You don't know 'bout hydrophoby skunks?'

'Never heard of 'em.'

'You do know about skunks, don't you?'

'Well, sure. But they just stink a lot. They kill chickens an' such, but they ain't nothin' to be afraid of. Unless you're close enough to get sprayed, that is.'

'That's true enough, unless they get an outbreak o' hydrophoby.'

'What's hydrophoby?'

'Rabies. Same thing that makes dogs rabid sometimes, don't you know?'

Andrew's eyes lighted up momentarily.

'Oh. Hydrophobia. Rabies. Skunks get that?'

'Oh, they not only get it, they get it bad. Once they get it, they start huntin' stuff they'd normally run from. Folks, especially. They'll chase down a person quicker'n a grizzly bear. An' it only takes one bite, an' the one they bite'll die a horrible death o' hydrophoby.'

'But doesn't it just kill the skunks, like it does a dog?'

'No, the skunks don't die from it. Not for a long while, anyway. They go on for a long while a-huntin' an' bitin' everythin' they can. Even each other, so it spreads like wild-fire. You get in an area o' hydrophoby skunks, you're gonna be the luckiest man in the world if you get out of it alive.'

Andrew silently filed the information away, deciding it

would be necessary to let the rest of the people in the wagon train know about the danger, lest they be as unaware as he himself had been. Little did he suspect that even in their extreme circumstances the mountain man was setting him up to be the butt of his joke.

As they skirted the lake in the next valley hundreds of ducks rose into the air, filling Andrew's ears with the sound of their wings.

'I've never seen so many ducks,' he commented.

On a fairly level spot high enough to be away from most of the mosquitoes and biting flies, a place where the wind had a clear sweep, further hindering the insects, Wilson stepped from the saddle.

'Gettin' dark now that the moon's down. We gotta stop till daylight. The horses need to graze a while anyway.'

Andrew chafed at the announcement, biting his tongue lest he offend the leader of their pursuit. He couldn't completely contain himself, though.

'Won't they get farther ahead of us?'

'Maybe. Can't be helped. If I miss the trail in the dark, we'll have a deuce of a time findin' it again. If he's figured out we're followin', he can lay up in the dark an' bushwhack us. And, like I already tol' you, we gotta take care o' the horses. They're life an' death in this country. If your horse is in good shape, so are you.'

It had been a terribly long and taxing day. Andrew thought he had scarcely rolled into his blankets when Wilson's toe nudged him awake.

'Sunup's just over an hour away,' he announced. 'Coffee's on.'

Andrew turned out of his blankets, rolled up his bedding

and secured it to the back of his saddle. He accepted with gratitude the steaming cup of strong coffee the mountain man handed him.

'I didn't even think to grab any coffee,' he apologized. 'Sure glad you did.'

'I try to never leave anywhere without bein' ready to stay for a month or two if I have to,' Wilson replied. 'I sure ain't gonna go that long without my coffee if I can help it.'

Before the sun dared to fully show its face they were in the saddle again. They had ridden less than an hour when Buck reined in, studying the trail ahead. They sat there a long while as he silently studied signs that only he could see.

'What's wrong?' Andrew eventually inquired.

Wilson did not respond, frowning as they approached a low saddle between valleys toward which the trail led.

Andrew found himself unable to remain silent in the face of the change in his mood.

'What's wrong?' he queried again.

Wilson just shook his head. Instead of staying on the trail, he turned abruptly at right angles away from it, riding directly toward the top of a nearby hill. Close to the top he repeated his habit of dropping from his horse, removing his hat, and crawling to the top of the hill. His head barely high enough to see through the tall grass, he studied the surrounding country for what seemed to Andrew like an hour. In reality it was a fourth of that.

Wilson returned to his horse and mounted again. He rode back to their quarry's trail, but crossed it instead of following it. At the top of another hill he repeated his previous action. He walked back to his horse.

'What did you see?' Andrew demanded.

Wilson pursed his lips. 'Looks like they stopped for the night.'

'How long did they stop?' Andrew asked, implications of that information clamoring in his mind.

'Can't tell. No fire. Nothin'. Looks like they just stopped, lay down separate for a while, then up an' left again. Just waitin' for daylight, likely.'

'Separately?' Andrew echoed, his voice betraying the intensity of his emotion.

'Looks like. Not enough trampled grass for anythin' else to've gone on.'

Andrew frowned, unsure whether to believe Wilson. He was also unwilling to doubt the information, given the surge of hope it ignited within him.

'Why separately, do you suppose? I mean that's a big relief, but it don't seem to fit.'

Buck eyed him closely, obviously understanding the drift of the questions the young man was unwilling to ask out loud.

'Anybody's guess,' he said at last. 'My best guess, knowing what a snake in the grass Smith is, is he's savin' her till he joins up with his Indian pals. Then he'll claim 'er as a wife in front o' everybody, just to show off.'

Andrew felt the blood drain from his face.

'He'd do that?'

'He'd do that,' Wilson confirmed. 'And worse, if he takes a notion.'

'What could be worse?'

Wilson studied him for a long moment before he answered. His voice was flat, as if seeing something in his memory that time had not purged.

'He could invite others to take turns on 'er when he's done,' he said.

Andrew found himself unable to answer. He could only mount his horse and wait impatiently for the mountain man to lead the way. They had to find their quarry before the barbaric renegade could meet up with the Arapaho friends toward whom he was presumably riding.

Even as he mentally recited that determination, a small voice in the back of his mind told him they would be too late, if they even found them at all.

CHAPTER 24

A kick in the ribs sent shocks of pain through Hannah's body, jerking her to wakefulness through a thick haze of sleep. The realities of the previous day surged upward in her mind. She struggled to her feet.

'Get on your horse,' Jeremiah Smith commanded. 'It's pertneart daylight.'

It was still dark enough for her to be barely able to make out the outline of her horse, standing saddled and ready, its lead rope once again secured in a loop around the neck of the mountain man's mount.

'Better do your chores afore you do, though,' he corrected himself. 'We ain't stoppin' again for a good long while.'

The humiliation of being watched while she emptied her bladder washed through Hannah. Even as it did, she recognized the wisdom of the crude command. She did need to do so. She would not have another opportunity until he saw fit.

Steeling herself against the repeated violation of her personhood, she complied. Fighting against an unexpected dizziness, she hurriedly mounted her horse, trying with all her might to ignore the leering grin of her captor. It was more than evident that he reveled in her embarrassment and humiliation. What further degradations he had in mind for her tortured her imagination. She fought against the images that hammered at her resolve to remain stoic and strong.

As he started to turn toward his own horse, Smith reached out a hand and offered her a dark-reddish-brown piece of something. As she took it she asked,

'What's that?'

'Jerky,' he replied. 'Don't want you passin' out an' fallin' off your horse 'cause you ain't ate nothin'.'

She realized with a start that she had eaten nothing since yesterday morning. Trying hard not to think how he came by the piece of dried meat or where he had been carrying it, she gnawed off a small piece of it and began to chew. As soon as she did so, hunger washed over her. It actually began to taste good, as the needs of her body overcame her repugnance.

As she chewed her mouth watered and began to soften the cured meat. Eventually she was able to chew it well enough to swallow the bite. She was suddenly ravenous. She ripped at the tough substance until she was able to tear off another, somewhat larger bite. She chewed on it a lot longer, savoring its strong flavor that would have been a total turn-off to her a couple months ago. She decided it must be venison. By the time she had begun working on her third bite she could sense a definite improvement in the way she felt. The faintness that had made her dizzy as she mounted her horse began to recede. In spite of her circumstances, she marveled at the strength a small amount of meat could impart to her weary, aching body.

They crossed the next two valleys without encountering any water in the bottoms. The ground ceased to be sand beneath a thin layer of sod, and became hard. The edges of the valleys steepened. Hard yellow clay formed frequent low cliffs, but by and large they continued to ride through low, rolling hills.

As they topped one ridge and started down the other side she saw higher hills, with a distinct greenish coloring, rise against the skyline to the north-west.

The valleys that, through the sandhills, had almost run east and west, now began to favor instead a north-south orientation. It was a change that was lost on Hannah until she realized they were simply following one of the valleys, but still riding generally northward.

As they rode the valley became more like a canyon, until it opened onto a wide valley that ran almost, once again, east and west. In the distance the sun reflecting off water indicated the presence of a good-sized river.

At first sight of the river she thought her captor grunted in satisfaction, but he was far enough ahead for her not to be sure.

She *was* sure how welcome the water was when they reached its edge. Her delight in the cold freshness of the water coursing down her throat was no less than that clearly displayed by the horses. She also knew the stop would require a repetition of the humiliation in which the renegade so obviously exulted. She was pleasantly surprised when he virtually ignored her this time, devoting his attention instead to their back trail.

Abruptly showing more urgency, he ordered her onto her horse. He took the time to offer her another piece of jerky, which she grasped eagerly. He leaped onto his horse's back and kicked him immediately into motion, parallel to the river, heading downstream.

The suddenness of the move caught Hannah's horse by surprise. As soon as he had drunk from the river he had begun to rip ravenously at the tall grass growing beside it. The hard, sudden tug of the lead rope nearly jerked him off balance, causing him to make three lunging jumps to catch up. No sooner had he done so than Smith steered his horse into the river, still maintaining a downstream angle.

As soon as both horses were well into the river, he turned his own mount back upstream. They animals were forced to swim almost at once. Smith slid off his horse and gripped its mane, letting his own body float along. Taking her cue from him, Hannah did the same, gripping her saddle horn with one hand and frantically holding on to the piece of jerky with the other.

As they neared the far shore the horses' hoofs found footing. Both riders, she following his lead, climbed back aboard. Instead of going ashore, however, Smith kept the animals well out into the river for more than a quarter-mile. When they came to a stretch of gravel where a side canyon opened into the river, he at last went ashore.

As soon as both horses were on solid ground he kicked

his horse into a gallop, forcing Hannah's horse to follow suit. He forced the mounts to their utmost speed until the sides of the wide wash deepened, and it curved so that they were no longer in sight of the river.

Both animals were breathing hard when he let them slow, but he continued at a quicker pace than they had maintained over the entire distance. For some reason that Hannah was unable to fathom, he was suddenly uneasy, acting almost as though afraid, casting frequent glances over his shoulder.

When a side canyon opened off the one they followed, he took it for half a mile. When they climbed out on the north side of that canyon, he paused near the top. Moving slowly he stretched as tall as he could, staring at their back trail. At one point he stood up on top of his horse, staring that direction. He continued to seem agitated until they had come out on top and moved down a long gentle slope far enough to be no longer visible to anyone behind them.

Before them the country changed amazingly. After not having seen a tree from the time they left the Platte River until they reached what she didn't know was the Niobrara River, they entered a terrain marked by pine timber and scrub cedars. Hills and canyons extended as far as she could see. The timber offered welcome shade, but she felt increasingly isolated.

They rode through increasingly rough and steep country until the sun was well west of its median. Hannah desperately needed to stop and relieve herself again, despite whatever humiliation it entailed. She had long since finished the second piece of jerky he had given her. She was so thirsty her tongue stuck to the roof of her mouth.

With no warning Smith jerked his horse to a halt. He

cocked his head to one side, listening intently. He jerked the reins on his horse, spinning him around, reversing his direction. Kicking the animal's sides furiously, he sped past Hannah, the lead rope immediately jerking her horse around and forcing him to follow.

'What … what is it?' she surprised herself by asking, her voice rasping through her parched throat.

'Shut up!' he ordered in a harsh whisper.

They raced back the way they had come. As they topped a rise and started down the other side she heard noises behind them that she could not identify. Only as the intervening hill cut off the sound did she realize they were human voices, shrill with pain or anger. They were punctuated by gunshots as well.

The pair of them rode as if the devil himself was on their trail, until a harsh voice yelled, 'Hold it right there!'

CHAPTER 25

'We're gettin' outa the sandhills.'

Andrew nodded. 'Yeah. Are we gettin' closer?'

'We're gainin'. I'm guessin' he ain't carryin' no grain for the horses, an' he ain't givin' 'em time to eat, or even to drink as often as he oughta. They're startin' to wear down.'

The day wore on past mid-morning. They stopped every hour or so, whenever a stream or pond afforded the opportunity to let the horses drink and themselves to do likewise. They gave both animals a small bait of oats each time, carefully conserving the stash of grain Wilson had brought so as to make it last. Even so their mounts began to signal their reluctance to start again after each stop.

They moved from the soft sandy footing beneath the thin cover of topsoil onto more solid ground. The gently rolling hills turned into longer stretches of flat land, punctuated by canyons along which occasionally steeper sides indicated where and when they could be breached.

The direction of the valleys changed from a generally east-west orientation to more north-northeast to south-southwest.

'The land's changin',' Andrew noted at one point.

'We're gettin' close to the Niobrara River valley,' Buck explained. 'All the draws an' canyons 'll lead to it now. Some way past it is Cottonwood Crick, then we'll be into the Wildcat Hills.'

'What are they?'

'That's the pine ridge, canyon country I mentioned to you once. It's a whole different kinda land. Timber. Mostly pine, with quite a bit o' scrub cedar thrown in. Deep canyons sometimes. Nice country. Not as much water as in the sand-hills, but at least it's got trees. I don't much cotton to country without trees.'

'Timber'll make it harder to see far.'

'It does that, all right. I ain't sure Smith is smart takin' his Arapahos into that country, though.'

'Why not?'

'It's Sioux country. Lakota. Them an' the Arapahos don't get along.'

'So why would the Arapahos go there?'

'Well, I can only guess. If I was to make a guess, it'd be

that the army's less likely to chase 'em down there. And if the army does manage to track 'em that far, they can hope the army'll stumble onto some Sioux instead, an' get all tied up in a fight with them.'

'What if it's them that run into the Sioux instead?'

'Well, if that happens, who knows what'll happen to Hannah. That's why we gotta catch up to 'em afore they get that far.'

The Niobrara River appeared before them well ahead of Andrew's guess. It both worried and excited him. It should mean they were closer to their quarry. It also meant Smith was closer to his goal. A sense of urgency made it difficult for him not to try to spur the mountain man to greater speed.

Instead of increasing their speed, Wilson seemed to slow. He grew ever more cautious. As they approached every stretch of open ground, he stopped and studied it carefully before crossing.

When the river came into their field of vision they were scarcely 300 yards from it. Buck dismounted and climbed to the top of a large outcrop of butte rock, a hard, almost white substance that formed the sides of the canyon from which they were about to emerge.

He quickly dropped to his knees, then scrambled down the side of the small butte he had climbed. He ran to his horse.

'I spotted 'em,' he said, 'but he mighta spotted me. Let's move.'

He touched his horse with his spurs for the first time that Andrew could remember. He didn't wear spurs, but he kicked his horse, who seemed more than willing to keep pace with Buck anyway. They came to the river and plunged directly into it, aiming for a gravel beach an eighth of a mile or more upstream.

Andrew was instantly confused. However, already experienced in crossing rivers, he slid out of the saddle and let his body float, hanging onto the saddle horn while his horse swam. When their horses' hoofs found solid ground on the far side they both moved back into the saddle.

As they gained the flat gravel bed of the wide draw, Andrew goaded his horse up alongside the mountain man's.

'Didn't I see tracks headin' downstream back there?' he asked.

'Hey! You're learnin' to watch tracks. Yeah. That was their tracks.'

'Then why aren't we goin' that way.'

''Cause where I spotted 'em was this way. I'm guessin' he made them tracks on account of he's either spotted us, or figures he might be followed. He's made it look like they went downstream, so if anyone is followin' 'em they'll spend a lot of time traipsin' the bank downstream lookin' for where they came out. But they came out right where we did.'

'You can see their tracks in this gravel?'

'Yeah. They ain't all that far ahead of us. The top o' some o' the rocks is wetter'n others. That means somethin' turned 'em over. Just like tracks in the grass.'

Spotting something that Andrew, again, was unable to see, Buck left the draw they were following and turned up another, smaller draw that opened off it. Half a mile further on he turned at right angles to climb up from the bottom of the draw and clambered up the relatively steep side. Before he gained the top he once again dismounted, removed his hat, and crawled to the top. Spotting a small scrub cedar, he rose to a crouch and peered through its branches, studying the area in front of him.

He returned to his horse without a word and finished riding up the side of the draw, entering a long slope that led to the beginning of the pine forest. They were scarcely into the trees when Buck threw up his hand, halting Andrew abruptly. He stood in his stirrups, listening intently. He whirled and whispered urgently,

'Comin' this way in a hurry!'

Andrew instantly wanted to ask the questions that leaped into his mind. *Who's coming? How do you know? Why are they in a hurry?*

Instead of asking any of them he responded to the leader's sense of urgency and followed him. They rode directly to the last draw from which they had climbed and hurried back into it. Instead of following it, Buck turned to ride up the draw and around a bend, out of sight. He dismounted, drawing his rifle from its saddle scabbard.

Totally bewildered, Andrew could think of nothing else to do, so he simply followed the mountain man's example. When Buck levered a shell into his rifle's chamber, Andrew did likewise.

In sight of the spot where they and, earlier, their quarry, had climbed from the draw, Buck flopped to the ground behind a group of large rocks. He motioned with his hand, indicating a similar spot for Andrew to crouch in. Still confused by the other's behavior, Andrew silently did as he was bidden.

They were in place scarce minutes before Andrew heard horses approaching rapidly. Almost at once Smith came into view. Behind him a few paces Hannah's horse emerged, with her hanging onto the saddle horn for dear life.

They slid and skidded down the side of the draw. Just as they reached the bottom Buck yelled,

'Hold it right there!'

As if slung from a spring, the renegade dived from his horse. He tucked his shoulder as he landed and rolled to his feet in one continuous motion. Dodging from one side to the other, instead of fleeing, he came straight toward the sound of the voice.

Buck fired quickly twice, missing with both shots. Then the renegade was on him, ramming a shoulder into him, driving him back and down. He sprang to his feet, a large knife in his hand as if it had apparated there magically.

Buck was on his own feet just as swiftly. He sidestepped the swift attack of Smith, the latter's knife blade just touching the midriff of Buck's garment. Buck lunged in just behind the knife's arc, aiming his own knife at the renegade's chest. The blade cut through the renegade's buckskin shirt just enough to nick the flesh beneath, but inadequately to do any damage.

Andrew stood with drawn pistol trained on the pair. He kept moving the weapon, trying to find a way to get a clear shot at the renegade without, more likely, killing his partner.

As if it were a planned move Smith's knife reversed and swept backward, aimed at Buck's throat. Buck ducked beneath it and lashed out with a foot, catching the would-be Arapaho behind the heel. As his foot was kicked out from beneath him the renegade went down. Instead of trying to regain his feet, he lashed out with one foot and caught Buck behind his right ankle, kicking the leg out from under him. As he fell, Buck's hand hit a large rock, dislodging his knife from his hand.

Seeing his advantage immediately, the renegade lunged onto his supine opponent. Grabbing him by the hair he slammed his head back against the ground, at the same time raising his knife high to plunge it into Buck's chest. Buck was helpless to prevent the fatal thrust.

The shot sounded unnaturally loud as it echoed back and forth from the walls of the narrow canyon. The renegade flew backward off Buck, to flop spread-eagled on the ground. Buck rolled to the side, retrieved his knife and rose to his knees, knife at the ready.

Jeremiah Smith, or Jeremiah Moses, or Harvey Ridley, or the turncoat outlaw by any other name, was beyond endangering anybody. Eyes wide, staring vacantly into space, he lay unmoving on the ground.

Buck whirled to look at Andrew. He stood spraddle-legged, holding his pistol in both hands, eyes far too wide open, his jaw sagging. A wisp of smoke drifted upward from his gun barrel. He snapped his mouth shut as he realized it was hanging open. He cleared his throat. He said, 'I … I couldn't get a clear shot till then.'

Buck grinned. 'Well, you did when it counted.'

As if suddenly released from invisible constraints, Hannah leaped from her horse and ran to Andrew, arms held wide in front of her.

'Oh Andrew, Andrew! Oh Andrew, how did you ever find us? Oh Andrew. Oh!'

Then she was in his arms. He found himself unable to force any words past the huge, hard lump in his throat. He just flung his arms around her and squeezed her, as if to draw her completely into himself. He buried his face in her

143

hair, tears flowing in small rivers down his face.

Neither of them saw Buck carefully clean the blood from his knife blade and replace it in its sheath. He retrieved his rifle and levered a fresh shell into the chamber. He turned to Andrew and Hannah.

'We gotta get a move on. We're a long way from outa the woods.'

Both of them turned a puzzled look on the inert mountain man.

'But ... but ... he's dead now,' Hannah said, as if trying to convince herself as much as Buck.

'He ain't the problem no more. He was runnin' from somethin', an' we'd better run too. I'm guessin' his bunch of Arapaho ran into the Sioux. That's the battle we just barely heard sounds of. That's why we turned around to beat-feet it back to here to be ready when you got this far. Whoever it is 'll be after us just as quick as they were after you two. They sure as anythin' heard us shootin', and they'll be ridin' here hell for leather. Let's move it!'

Only then did Andrew realize he still held his pistol in one hand. He swiftly replaced it in its holster and fastened the narrow leather loop that held it in place. He grabbed up his rifle from where he had dropped it on the ground. Within a minute or two they were all three back in the saddle, Buck leading the dead renegade's horse. None knew better than Buck that it would take a near miracle for them to outrun those certain to pursue them, almost as certainly Sioux. Their horses were spent. They were exhausted. Their chances of survival were slim indeed.

CHAPTER 26

The waters of the Niobrara River felt wonderfully cool and refreshing, but they dared not dally in their caress any longer than it took to swim to the other side. Buck led them into a thick stand of cottonwood trees and choke cherry bushes. He dismounted swiftly.

Racing back to the edge of the cover, he studied the far shoreline and the hills beyond. He nodded, knelt at the water's edge and drank deeply.

He stepped back into the cover and drew his rifle from its scabbard.

'You two go get a good drink, then water the horses,' he said. 'Give 'em all a good bait o' oats from my left saddlebag. I'll keep watch while you do.'

Realizing their time was extremely limited at best, Andrew and Hannah hastened to comply. Hannah had no hat to use to feed her horse any of the oats. Buck whipped his own hat off and tossed it to her.

'Give your horse an' Smith's twice as much,' he instructed, his eyes never ceasing in their sweep of the country beyond the river. 'I don't reckon Smith bothered to have any for 'em.'

'He didn't,' Hannah confirmed. 'They have to be as hungry as I am.'

As they finished their care of the horses and prepared to remount, Andrew handed Hannah two dried biscuits from his own saddle bag.

'These are harder'n rocks,' he said. 'Just stick 'em in the river for just a bit, then mount up. That'll soften 'em enough for you to get your teeth into 'em.'

Somehow it hardly seemed any different to Hannah to dip her food in the brownish water of the river from how it felt to drink that same water. She stifled her reluctance and did as Andrew bade her. They left the cover of the riverbank at a swift trot, Buck leading the riderless horse.

Half a mile along the broad canyon they had followed to the river, the mountain man veered to the side, where hard, rocky ground would make their trail difficult to see. They rode into the open at the top, heading at a swift gallop toward the next canyon to the west, where they could again drop low enough to be out of the field of vision of searching eyes.

All the way across that three-quarters of a mile of open ground the hair on the back of their necks bristled and tingled. They could almost hear the triumphant whoops of pursuing Indians.

Something of their fear seemed to be transmitted to the horses. They responded more willingly than their exhausted state should have dictated. In short order they plunged over the side of that other canyon, sliding and skidding their way to the bottom.

The bottom of that gully was nearly an eighth of a mile across. It was lush with tall grass. Patches of choke cherry bushes, plum bushes, buckbrush and various other bushes were scattered everywhere. The hungry horses continually reached down and snatched mouthfuls of the tall grass, already headed out and heavy with seed. As they trotted along they munched it as best they could with the bits in their mouths. At least they gained some nourishment from it. Their riders all knew it would likely not be enough.

Because the moon rises nearly an hour later each day, it was high in the sky by the time the sun was tucked behind the southern tip of the Wildcat Hills to their west. They had come out onto open ground, rolling hills broken by broad expanses of prairie grasses. Trees became more and more scarce.

From time to time they crossed small streams fed by springs. At each one they stopped, drank, grabbed food from their saddlebags to munch while they rode, and refilled the two canteens they had between them. For Hannah, exhausted as she was, it seemed like heaven by comparison to the way she had been led on the ride northward. For Andrew it was simply taxing and tense. He was sure he could hear sounds of the pursuit of Indians behind them wafting on every breeze. What passed through the mountain man's mind was for him alone to know, as he gave no indication.

'We'll stop here,' he announced several hours later. They were at another of the small streams that crossed their paths. The moon had set, plunging the land into near total darkness.

Buck selected a low hollow half a mile from the creek. They hobbled the horses, who began ravenously to tear off great mouthfuls of the abundant grass. Buck built a small fire and started a pot of coffee.

'We'll fry some bacon an' eat good,' he said. 'We're gonna likely need all the strength we can get afore this thing is done.'

In minutes the smell of frying bacon wakened the stifled hunger of three over-taxed fleers from an unseen enemy whom they well knew to be on their trail.

'Maybe they'll just be happy Smith is dead when they find

his body,' Andrew hoped aloud, 'and not bother to chase after whoever killed 'im.'

'They'll be after us,' Buck assured him. 'We invaded their territory just as surely as the band of Arapahos did. They don't take kindly to that. The Wildcat Hills are on the south-western end o' their territory, but they're mighty particular about who traipses around in it. It's great huntin' country for them. There's deer an' elk an' buffalo an' all kinds o' small game that's easy huntin' for 'em. With all that timber an' all, they can creep up close to most anything. It's likely a huntin' party that run onto the Arapahos. That means it's all warriors. No women. No kids. So they can up an' follow us as long as they want to make sure we don't come back into their huntin' ground.'

They ate as if they were starving, supplementing the freshly fried bacon with dried biscuits dunked in the scalding coffee. No feast ever tasted so grand to Hannah. Even as she finished her food sleepiness overwhelmed her. It was all she could do to wrap up in one of Andrew's blankets before she was sound asleep.

'You'n me'll stand watch,' Buck informed Andrew, 'in two-hour spells. Set yourself up against that clump o' brush right up there on top o' the knoll. Make sure you don't drop off to sleep. Listen more'n you watch. If they're on our trail an' close, an' they keep movin' when it's this dark, they'll make enough noise you'll hear 'em a long time afore you see anything.'

Andrew nodded, picked up his rifle and moved to his assigned post. He fought off his fatigue by remembering his fear for Hannah. He pondered the feelings of triumph and euphoria, mingled with revulsion that had assailed him when he shot the renegade. It was the first time he had shot at a human being, let alone killing someone.

A coyote howled into the darkness. The call was instantly answered by three others from varied points of the compass. A rustle of wings passed above him. He supposed it must be an owl, but it was too dark to identify it. Small sounds betrayed the activity of small animals. He stayed alert by trying to identify what they might be.

When something, possibly a raccoon, caught a mouse, the mouse's brief squeak was cut off almost before it began. It seemed far longer than two hours before Buck appeared, approaching in total silence.

'My turn,' he announced. 'Go grab some shuteye.'

Andrew lay down almost against Hannah and pulled his blanket over him. He had barely closed his eyes, he thought, before Buck said,

'Your turn again.'

Reluctantly Andrew returned to his post. It was much more difficult than before to stay awake and alert. He was nodding off when a strange sound in the darkness jerked him to wakefulness. He was sure he heard footsteps approaching. He strained his eyes and ears. He raised his rifle, pointing it at nothing in particular, his finger on the trigger.

Something moved in the darkness a dozen yards to his left. He whipped his rifle around. He fought the urge to fire into the darkness. Fear raised its call to panic deep within him. He considered yelling for Buck, but was afraid to betray his presence and position to whatever was out there. His breathing was rapid, as if he had run a long distance. His heart pounded.

Strain as he might, he heard nothing more. After a long while he began to relax.

'Must've been some critter huntin' in the dark,' he assured himself.

Again it seemed far more than two hours later when Buck appeared to relieve him. Once more he was asleep almost before he had his blanket pulled over himself.

It was still dark when Buck nudged him awake. He sat up abruptly, grabbing his rifle that lay at his side.

'Time to start movin',' the mountain man announced.

Rubbing the sleep from his eyes, Andrew noticed that the small fire was already burning. As he did he recognized the smell of coffee and bacon once again cooking.

He nudged Hannah, sleeping beside him. She stirred reluctantly, mumbling something unintelligible. He nudged her again.

'Wake up, sweetheart,' he said, daring to speak the term he had seldom dared to use with her. 'We gotta get movin'.'

As wakefulness intruded on whatever dream brought the slight smile to her lips, her eyes flew open. Stark fear receded as she recognized Andrew and remembered her rescue. She suddenly felt an urgent need to relieve herself.

Grateful for the darkness and the greater consideration of her companions, she completed the necessary routine swiftly and returned to the fire. Within less than half an hour they had completed their breakfast, saddled the horses, and were prepared to resume their flight.

At breakfast Buck offered another surprise that amazed them. From a small jar secreted in his saddlebag he poured honey onto each of their biscuits, already softened in the scalding coffee.

'I always carry a bit o' honey when I can,' he explained. 'There ain't nothin' like it for quick energy when you're plumb hard up for anythin' to eat.'

He was right. Both Andrew and Hannah were amazed at the change in their energy levels by the time they had completed breakfast and prepared to ride.

They returned to the creek to water the horses and refill their canteens once again. The water was clear and cold. Both they and their horses demonstrated their appreciation by the quantity they consumed.

The sun was still fully half an hour from showing itself, but the ambient light was adequate to illuminate their way. They started off at a brisk trot.

By noon they began to feel more at ease. Whatever pursuit there might have been must have been left behind. None the less they rode cautiously, keeping to low-lying ground whenever possible, bearing almost due south, desperate to reach the Oregon Trail where they might expect friendly folks to bolster whatever defense they were forced to mount.

Just after noon Buck climbed a lone elm tree, growing inexplicably on top of a low knoll. He scrambled back down more quickly than he had climbed up. He looked around with an urgency instantly apparent to both Andrew and Hannah.

'What's wrong?' Andrew demanded.

'They're comin',' Buck announced, 'They got one eager-beaver tracker that's almost on us.' He jerked his rifle from its scabbard and returned to the tree. 'You two ride down there. Keep quiet. Take my horses with you. Be ready to ride when I come a-runnin'.'

Andrew and Hannah complied, staying where they were generally out of sight but where they could clearly see the mountain man. He positioned himself behind the trunk of the big elm he had climbed, resting his rifle against it, watching along the top of the barrel.

He had been in position only minutes when the head and shoulders of an Indian appeared, riding toward them, eyes cast down to the ground as he followed their trail. At the report of Buck's rifle he threw up his hands. His rifle flew off toward his right. He fell backward off his horse. The animal bolted forward several leaps, then stopped in confusion. Buck whirled and raced to his horse, leaping into the saddle.

'Move!' he ordered, jamming his spurs to the animal's sides.

The startled animal was running at full speed in half a dozen jumps. It would have taken fewer, but the riderless horse Buck led was slower to respond. Andrew and Hannah were close behind.

They ran all out for nearly half an hour, keeping to the low ground just as much as possible. They heard no pursuer behind them, but they knew he was there. The tracker would not have been alone, nor very far ahead of the rest of whatever war party followed.

At a stretch of hard, bare ground, Buck turned at right angles to their path of flight. Keeping where they would leave no tracks, the trio rode at a fast trot for nearly a mile before once again turning south. They knew the Indians would decipher the tactic, but it would take them a while. Maybe long enough. Probably not.

'How far is it to the trail?' Hannah asked at one point.

Buck pointed. 'Fifteen, twenty miles. Look over thataway and you can just make out Chimney Rock.'

'Fifteen or twenty miles yet?' Andrew responded, fear and despair giving sharp edges to his words.

Whatever answer Buck might have offered was cut off by the sounds that drifted to their ears. Less than half a mile behind them a chorus of whoops and hollers announced their pursuers had spotted them.

'Move!' Buck shouted once again.

This time the horses sensed the urgency, and were all running flat out almost at once. Buck in the lead followed the path that offered the fewest obstructions, intent now only on trying to outstay the stamina of their pursuers' horses. Even as they did, they knew the odds were heavily against them.

The distance between them and their pursuers remained almost constant. If anything, the pursuing Indians were gaining ground on them. Almost two miles from the beginning of the chase Andrew could feel his horse beginning to falter. He maintained the pace, but his gait became noticeably more labored.

Hannah's horse was in even worse condition. It had suffered more neglect from the renegade mountain man on their flight northward, and had less in reserve from which to draw.

As despair began to creep into his mind, Andrew began to envision worst-case scenarios. He would not, could not, allow Hannah to fall into the Indians' hands. But how could he prevent it? They could fight it out, but it was obvious they were badly outnumbered. If it came down to a time of utter despair, would he have the fortitude to kill her to spare her the tortures of captivity? Or, if to kill her, then to kill himself? Or would Buck deal with that? If he too hadn't already been killed by that time.

Suddenly Buck changed course, turning toward a tall butte. Its steep walls of white butte rock appeared insurmountable. At the base of the butte huge chunks of the rocklike clay boulders lay strewn about.

Just behind that cluster of boulders there appeared to be a hollow, possibly ten or twelve feet deep. Following their leader, they rode into that hollow at a full run.

Buck leapt from the saddle and ran to the edge of the cluster of boulders. Dropping prone, he sighted along the length of his rifle barrel.

Following his lead, Andrew did the same, motioning Hannah to lie flat on the ground. The Indians had not slackened their pace, approaching with terrifying speed.

'Don't shoot till I do,' Buck commanded.

Andrew loosened his grip on the trigger, which he had been about to squeeze. Then Buck's rifle barked. The lead Indian flopped from his horse. Andrew drew a bead on one of the attackers and squeezed the trigger. Buck fired a second time almost at the same instant as Andrew. Both bullets found their marks.

Those remaining of the band of Indians swerved to the side. Every one of them dived from his horse and disappeared in the long grass.

'Watch the grass,' Buck ordered. 'When you see grass movin', shoot right at the spot where it's wigglin''

Even as he spoke he fired. From the grass a little over 200 yards away they heard the unmistakable thwack of the leaden projectile slamming into flesh.

Andrew fired at what he thought was movement in the grass, but heard no evidence of a hit.

Bullets began to chip away at the butte rock boulders in which they had sought cover. Arrows smacked the ground around them.

'Keep 'em busy,' Buck ordered. 'I gotta get the horses down flat or they'll figure out a way to shoot them. I'll bring more ammunition back with me.'

Andrew did not answer while the mountain man crawled backward until he could stand in a crouch. He went to the horses. One by one he lifted a front leg, then eared them over until they fell flat. He swiftly tied the legs of each so they couldn't rise. He gave Hannah Jeremiah Smith's rifle.

'Here,' he said. 'You know how to shoot this?'

'Yes ...' she said hesitantly. 'But not very well.'

'Just keep it cocked and ready. If anyone comes sneakin' around behind us, shoot in their general direction at least. When I hear you shoot, I'll come runnin'.'

'O ... OK,' she stammered.

Not waiting for any further response he moved quickly back beside Andrew. Andrew fired at a spot where he thought the grass was moving. He was rewarded by more feverish movement in the grass.

'You got close or else nicked 'im,' Buck commented. 'He's movin' back outa range.'

'At least the ground's all bare close to us,' Andrew observed. 'They can't get very close and still stay in the grass.'

'Yeah, but we ain't got that much daylight left,' the mountain man quashed his optimism. 'In a couple hours they'll be able to slip right in on us afore we see or hear 'em.'

'Ain't there still a full moon?'

'Yeah, but it's too clouded over to help a whole lot.'

Andrew looked up at the overcast sky with a sinking feeling.

Sporadic firing marked the remainder of daylight. From time to time, following Buck's instructions, Andrew would raise his hat above the shelter of the rocks on the end of his rifle barrel. He had a couple bullet holes in it to attest to the accuracy of at least some of the Indian's marksmanship. Each time Buck would fire three shots in rapid succession at the spot where gunsmoke betrayed a hidden foe. He fired once at the spot, then once on either side of it. Only with one shot was he certain he had hit someone, but he mentally subtracted at least that one from the odds against them.

As the sun settled into the west and the ambient light began to dim, so also did their hopes. Mentally each of the three made plans for dealing with the coming onslaught that they knew was inevitable.

Suddenly the sound of a military trumpet split the air, sounding the command to charge. As if a bomb had landed in their midst Indians erupted from the grass, sprinting back to where one of their number held their horses, out sight of the besieged party.

Gunfire exploded from dozens of rifles away to their right. More than half the Indian ponies became suddenly riderless. At a second volley a couple more riders and three horses went down. The rest were quickly out of range. Half a dozen more shots rang out, but served only as a 'and don't come back' signal to the few survivors.

Blue uniformed soldiers appeared in a long line, guns at the ready, searching through the tall grass for any remaining Indians. They physically checked the bodies they came across, to ensure that no survivors remained to surprise them. A man in officer's uniform strode into the open.

'Hello the party in the rocks,' he called out.

'Hello yourself,' Buck answered instantly. 'Boy, are you ever a welcome sight! How'd you find us?'

'Lieutenant Daniel P. Woodbury, at your service, sir.' He strode to their position and extended his hand. Buck grasped it eagerly, shaking it far more effusively than was normal.

'You were making enough noise for a deaf mute to find you,' the officer explained. 'Do you have dead or wounded?'

'No, sir. Three souls, hale and hearty, thanks to you.'

'And who might you be?'

'Buck Wilson, with Andrew Stevenson and Hannah Henford, from Frank Cross's wagon train.'

'Is she the one that Ridley fellow kidnapped?'

'Yes, sir. She's the one.'

'What about Ridley?'

'He's dead. Andrew shot 'im dead, he did.'

'What about his Arapahos? They're the ones we've been most interested in.'

'Don't know, but I'm guessin' there ain't much left of 'em. We didn't see it, but we heard a good-sized battle goin' on. Smith, or Ridley, or whatever his name was, still had the girl. He was runnin' back south for all they was worth when we surprised 'em. I'm guessin' a huntin' party o' Sioux stumbled onto 'em an' pretty well took care o' that problem. I missed Smith a couple times afore Andrew plugged 'im. Then the Sioux came after us, 'cause they heard us shootin'. We lit out as fast as we could, an' managed to keep ahead of 'em until today. We was plumb outa time an' luck though, when you showed up. How'd you know to be headin' up this way?'

'We eventually figured out the Arapaho just faked headin' south, an' headed north instead. We been ridin' a path parallel to the trail to cut across their sign. We'd just run onto it when we heard the shootin' over here. Our scouts led us up where we could slip up on their flank without their knowin' we was in the area. One fine day for the United States army, and for the safety of the Oregon Trail, I do believe.'

Three souls faint with joy and relief agreed wholeheartedly.